The
Permanent History
Of Penaluna's Van

The
Permanent History
Of Penaluna's Van

By

Myrna Combellack

Date of Publication:
2003

Limited edition
/300

Published by:
Cornish Fiction 2003

Printed by:
ProPrint
Riverside Cottage
Great North Road
Stibbington
Peterborough PE8 6LR

ISBN: 0-954 1918-1-1

Cover drawing by Rob Wheeler

To better luck next time

ACKNOWLEDGEMENTS

Recognisable lines and imagery of William Blake; JP Donleavy; TS Eliot; Andrew Marvell.

'Oh life of this our spring! Why fades the lotus of the water,
Why fade the children of the spring, born but to smile and
fall?'

Blake: The Book of Thel

CHAPTER 1

The sun shines down on Toldhu Estate for the first time in half a year. One or two windows open and even the children yelling in the school yard seem revived.

Marjorie squeezes through the doorway, puffs up the passage, sits down at one of the kitchen chairs and regards Lois, who married the Swede.

'These combs break in yer hair. They don't make nothin' right these days. They put somethin' in the water too. When I 'ave a bath I git itchy. Look at my legs.'

'What do you put in the water, Marjorie?'

'Nothin'. I 'ave a bath every day, so I don't put nothin' in. I think it's bathin' so much, I get these great red spots. I been boilin' my towels. I'll have to see the doctor, 'spose.

'Will you have a drink, Marjorie?'

'Oo 'es.'

'There's a choice of Sauternes and Bordeaux.'

'Give us a glass of Bordeaux. Does yer 'usband drink red wine now?'

'No, it's all lager here. This bottle is mine. He's gone back to where he came from. I don't think he can stand Toldhu Estate for very long. I think it confuses him.'

'What sort of place is Sweden, then?'

'Hard to say, Marjorie. Come out there with me next time. Then you'll see what I mean.'

'You 'aven't never said.'

'Yes I have. It's hard to say.'

'Alright. It's 'ard to say. The 'ouse is big, the livin' room is sunk, he got too much money an' you pay for everythin' in blood. What more do you want?'

'I get family allowance paid to me in pound notes here.'

'God, you are greedy, Lois. What a way of lookin' at things. And you got five children. Still, you got yer freedom.

Which is more than me. But then, what would I do with it if I had it now, with my weight?'

'Ruin yourself, Marjorie.'

'O God. Well, I'll 'ave to go an' see if old Penaluna's back. 'Ee's gone to Gweek with a washin' machine I thought I was to 'ave. I'll jes' 'ave another glass an' go. Nobody would 'ave me now, anyway.'

'Don't believe it, Marjorie. Don't believe it, Marjorie.'

'Thanks.'

CHAPTER 2

Toldhu Estate was built just before they finally learned how to build cheap houses on hillsides. All the ladies sitting behind glass, behind net. The sun quietly unjamming the swollen wood, this green March morning.

On the doorstep, laughing, cleaning a row of shoes, the biggest first, the teeniest last.

'Come on in, Marjorie.'

'How's the crack in the kitchen?'

'Past the pencil mark.'

Marjorie on her way, sideways down the hall, looking up at the ceilings, the walls, clucking, biting a thumbnail, frowning at the plaster.

'Yeah, it's pretty bad. You want to sell up quick. They'm building stronger ones up the other side. You could get another mortgage. They got a different sort of plaster over there, the sort that do move with the building, like.'

'God, Marjorie, I still owe Marshall Ward four hundred quid.'

'You'd never know it, the way you do dress.'

The baby crawled out of the linen cupboard, howling, steam rising from its towelling baby suit. Marjorie boiled a kettle in the kitchen. Lois stooped down, picking up the little infant, pulling off its clothes. Marjorie yawned. Lois advancing on the domestic boiler, kicking the toolbox. Lois working, hot water everywhere, dribbling into the cupboard, spreading across the floor.

'For God's sake, Lois, what the 'ell is happening?'

'Plumbing, Marjorie.'

'The bleddy water's everywhere. At least switch the 'lectric off.'

'Don't worry about it, Marjorie. Just a little repair. I squeezed a tube of instant rubber stuff around the washer this morning early, but it hasn't done the trick. It's this damned hot water. Jesus, what I could do with a man around here.'

'You clever bugger. I thought you wanted something.'

'Get Penaluna, will you?'

'Alright. I'll be back with the old fool.'

'Quick, Marjorie.'

Marjorie panted up Forth Vean into deserted Tolwhele Close. Penaluna, in gardening corduroys, leaned on a spade, the onions all underground. Greenhouse all kicked in, the clever little heater taken indoors after the fogs of November. Marjorie, stooping to meet the eye of ginger moustache.

'Good morning, or is it good afternoon, my love. 'Ome again, my 'andsome?'

Marjorie taking the measure of him.

'Good afternoon my love. Lois needs your help.'

'What's the trouble? Right away.'

Penaluna, wiping fairly clean hands on spotless corduroys, not moving an inch.

'Is it plumbing or gardening, now?'

'Plumbing, if I'm right.'

'Wha's the matter, then?'

Marjorie, weighing Penaluna, eyes upon the broken glass, which glints and winks.

'You 'aven't got the time, have you?'

'Certainly I got time. Wha's the matter?'

'You haven't got time.'

'I 'ave got time. Where 'ave I got to go?'

'You 'aven't got the time, have you?'

Penaluna, ripping off his over-corduroys in the garden. Marjorie goes indoors, smiling and humming, opening a bottle. Penaluna, off down the road, talking to himself.

'And wha's the trouble, then?'

'It's stopped now. The washer needs replacing.'

Penaluna with broad grins and winks. Terrible time of the year for it. Plumbing always goes when you least expect. Just as you're home and dry.

'Well, thankyou very much for coming down, your kind advice and good day to you, Mr Penaluna.'

In the cupboard, Lois wiping and mopping, the baby sopping up the wet corners with its new towelling babysuit.

'How do you ever manage here without a man, Lois? Fancy doing that nut up on your own. I never seen a woman work like you.'

'I've seen women run farms on their own, Mr Penaluna, lambing in the snow, brambles to the door, hacking their way out to greet the bread van. This place is a dollies-house. There's nothing here to go wrong.'

Penaluna walks around the house, looking for cracks.

'What made you buy a silly little 'ouse 'ere, then?'

'Place to live. It gets cold in the field.'

'What does He think about it, then?'

'Don't know. Swedes are too tall to think, in my experience.'

'All I ever wanted was to travel. My grandfather and 'is four brothers died out in South Africa. Went with the Henry Norse Gold Mining Company, they did. Lost every one of them out there. Course, then I got married instead, so that finished me. I wanted a proper life, work around the world a bit, but I wasn't to have that. I was a proper little singer and I could dance a bit too, but all tha's gone now. I can't do any of that now. Yes, I could sing and dance, one time. My father used to sing in the chapel choir up Wesley ~ Toldice Wesley.'

Everybody sang in the choir up Toldice Wesley.

'Now I got a house and a garden an' I got to work in ut.'

'Nothing like it.'

Marjorie's shadow across the threshold, bouncing in the doorway, indicating Penaluna's house and garden with her thumb. Penaluna sloping off to the onions. Settling down in the armchair by the window.

'Lois, ever 'eard tell of anybody having trouble getting it in?'

'Fat people.'

'I've never had a lot of opportunity, you know.'

'Yes, well don't ask me about it. I've never looked anything but hungry, which is what I am, most of the time. The only thing I look forward to in bed is breakfast. Give me a library card and I'll get out the biggest food book they've got. Doesn't help. I must be attractive to the men. Somebody always trying to get it up.'

''Asn't a man ever resisted your attractions?'

'Oh yes. Up there in Sheepwash. One of the 'uncles' got the idea in his head that he could be my father. That was the end of Mother's romance. I was young and impressionable at the time. I never got over it, and Mother hardly ever spoke to me again.'

'Terrible.'

'I was pretty ugly then. That was always the trouble with me, skinny and ugly. I never liked any men as such. Sometimes their conversation is mildly interesting. The only answer to any of it is old age.'

'I doubt it, Lois. There's always a catch, 'owever you do look at things.'

'Yeah? Just watch me grow old. Youth can nod off. All I want is peace. No more men, no more children, just me and the deckchair in the back garden, my golden privet all grown up. How can you live with Penaluna?'

'I've always lived with Penaluna.'

'You're finished if you talk like that.'

'Any'ow, what's your husband gone for? Politics? Trying to sell somethin'?'

'Sometimes he needs a little holiday.'

'One a these days 'ee'll see through you. 'Ow d'you get 'im t' pay you so much? I don't know 'ow you do git away with it. Penaluna do even take my dole away from me.'

'Well, I take him aside on the telephone and say, look, buster, I've paid this and that and I can't manage any more. I'll have to slit my throat.'

'You ought to live in Flen with 'im, though. 'Ee must 'ave a lot a money, 'Ee's got a room full of model railways, you said. Don't you know any more'n t' live over 'ere?'

'It's too late now, Marjorie. All that's gone. It was decided on the wedding night. No lady can hide her deepest feelings when the continental quilt has been kicked right off the bed in winter. He stayed here a full seven days, though, I'll say that for him.'

Marjorie pours the boiling water into the teapot.

'Yeah, 'ee's no fool. 'Ee can come an' go from Lunnun any time he feels like it. All he 'as t' do is keep you 'appy with a few thousand quid a year. You 'aven't made any profit. You'm still stuck 'ere on Toldhu Estate with no way out. All you got' do is git a grey 'air an' you'm finished. Or another kid.'

'Come on, Marjorie, everything is perfect. I've got children, a house, money, clothes and I don't have to live with anybody.'

'I'll pour yours first. I need a strong one.'

Marjorie pouring the tea from the pot. Sky darkening outside, the children all indoors. Penaluna's van straining up Cox Hill with last week's broccoli and fruit from foreign parts. Quietness in the house, the baby asleep in its lukewarm suit.

'You got trouble, Lois. To my way of thinkin', you got trouble. You'll end up with nothin' and nobody. You married right, an' 'ee's payin' now, but what about later, when he gits sick of it? You should live with 'im or git 'im to' live with

7

you. You'll git attracted to some kid in the supermarket an' then you'll be expectin' again. Then it'll be the divorce court an' not a penny to yer name, but a soddin' greet mortgage all yer own. You'll be stuck on Toldhu Estate for good then, an' the 'ouse gittin' old an' fallin' down.'

A pizza thawing, taken out of the cellophane and placed very carefully upon the grill pan. The temperature knob all set, in Celsius.

'Well, we'll have a little something before the boys get in from the cinema. Then I'll roast that piece of pork. This house is alright, really, until people start talking next door. Takes away all the privacy.'

'I c'n believe that.'

'Well, I don't like listening to other people's troubles. If she next door hasn't got enough cash to live on until the end of the week, I get very concerned for her. It increases the small number of worries I have. I like to have a peaceful time, thinking that everybody can pay their bills around here. The people who lived there before these, well he had a lot of problems he used to shout about. A very discontented man altogether. And the things he made her do for him, and she wasn't all that young, neither. I moved myself and all the kids into the spare room on the other side of the house. He wanted to come round here too. Silly old fool. He deserved what he got from me. When I leave Toldhu Estate, I shall be dressed in cream, with navy accessories, I'll click the latch shut for the last time, then I'll swish down the hill in my cream Mercedes, pausing only to turn the key once in the starter. At the end of the road, I shall glide into the traffic, looking neither left nor right. Everything will stop, not for tea, but for only me. The Swede will stand at the roadside, red and gawping. I shall fling my family allowance book in his face with a final backward glance of pure unconcern. The traffic wardens at the roundabout will pause and touch their hats. All the little children, including these, will smile and wave goodbye. Next day, from my hotel overlooking Central Park I shall write to Tage and say, "My dear boy, you have been a swine since the day you asked me my name, pushing me, my baby and my five suitcases through the swing doors onto the Gothenburg Ferry. I never liked you then and I never will now. You are what the Cornish mean by real hopeless. I will never forget you. Your loving wife, Lois." '

Marjorie laughing, her arms above her head, raising a brassiere strap to its rightful place on her shoulder, easing the elastic corselette around her fat stomach, a Cornish woman in her prime. Lois couldn't do it. She was at the pinnacle of her career. Lois wouldn't leave the children for five minutes.

'My God, he hates me. I think he hates me more than his mother does. She used to peep through the keyholes, and those bedrooms were full of doors. I stopped them up with bits of bread. And she kept throwing away my clothes. Sitting in the Wedgewood blue and white drawing-room: "Lois, the Umburra pot is full of Marks and Spencer underwear." What a way to treat a bride. The kids kept drowning in the pool. I preferred life in Tregajorran with my cousin Davey: "Get yer knickers off, Lois, I don't like they adverts on ITV." Over the broad back of the kitchen table before and after milking. A fine outdoor life. Pasties every Saturday and stew every other day. Where have the years gone? Still, it doesn't do to look back too fondly. Nothing was easy there either. Animals and mud everywhere. Teaching was a far finer profession, as you can imagine, and decently paid. But I was always poor. Nobody wants to learn a northern European language. To think I left Davey to perfect Swedish grammar and married a native speaker. Well, I can't say I learned much in Sweden. I need more practice. But not on him, no, that's for sure.'

'Go back to Davey, Lois.'

'The Cornish men are no good for marrying, Marjorie. Look at old Penaluna. Be honest about it, old girl, you wouldn't wish your life on me. It would be asking for trouble. And Davey has got a sort of wife.'

'I don't know what's good for you, Lois. You got more trouble than Penaluna got daisies. Your life is like Spot Odgers eating treacle. Go and join a club for single people. Get out and about a bit. Get a steady man.'

'Get this pizza down you. Your anxiety for me is taking pounds off you.'

'Lois, the pizza is superb. You'll 'ave to tell me about this selective buyin' of yourn.'

The mean, year-old, confused pizza, cold in its heart, toasted and curled at its crust, simmering on the plate which is a potter's second. The cooker creaking, its heat caressing the chilly plaster of the kitchen walls. Outside, the wind rises and cuts through the golden privet, and it seems that half my life I have been peeling the cellophane from pizzas and running into town for more of them. And the way home is always fraught with hills. And once, in high Edinburgh, an Egyptian waiter caught my eye, tearing off a piece of paper which is my bill, demanding my room number, when I looked down at my undecorated hands and the key, which was bold as brass, told me sixty-nine, my fate. And the self, replete, with forty years left to match the number on the card, there was all the time in the world to tiptoe through the red carpet and slide the key in the lubricated lock, which turned with a practised click. And how we laughed and laughed, Marjorie and me, the tears running down our faces, of how the Cornishwoman rode the Kamal out of Egypt in the ages gone, the babies looking up from their toys, star-eyed, my pearls of great price. Before this blond person, this Tage, who was taller than even me, and had hands which were stronger than mine, fine white hands with blond hair. In Flen, drinking strong cups of coffee, behind gingham curtains, the thunder and rain coming out of the northern sky at nine every morning, regarding me with slate-grey eyes, through cigarette smoke. Marry me, Lois. No. Thankyou. I couldn't. There are my children. And there is Davey and my life in Britain. There are the animals and there is the Carn. The way the rock stands on the hillside which is ours and ours alone. And the hard hand with the fine hairs, fine blond hairs, pressed passing over my belly.

'You're some quiet, Lois.'

'Marjorie, inquisitive, gnawing at the pizza, pieces of cheese all over the place and the tablecloth.

'Don't you know? Don't you hear it when I start to think? It's all hell in here; and out there, beyond the brain-case, it's quiet as Centenary Chapel without hymn books. Nature is a wonderful thing, remarkably quiet.'

'Well dear, I shouldn't let the past upset me. I never let Penaluna get to me. You got t' be thick-skinned in this world. No good to brood on it.'

'Oh for God's sake, Marjorie. Brood on what?'

'Brood on nothin', dear.'

'Finish your pizza.'

'Well, Lois, all of it's a big trap. Even a natural thing like eatin'. The greatest pleasure of all, accordin' to you.'

'Let's enjoy this and talk about the traps afterwards. The crack's a long way past the pencil mark.'

Young Keith racing down the hallway.

A six inch blade in his hand, young Keith prowling up the passage, waving it around at the kitchen door. Lois, positioned between the thug and Marjorie, her back to her son, seeing the small terror in Marjorie's eyes.

'Don't be frightened of old Penaluna, Marjorie. He's more terrified of you than you are of him. A little maladjusted, I'd say,' winking reassurance to her friend who has no children, the boy lashing the air.

'Oh well, if tha's all it is. I'll finish wha's on me plate an' toddle off 'ome.'

The knife lunged. Lois' arm swung, spinning round, pushing the boy clear, the door banging against the wall. Keith gasping, letting out a small cry.

'Jesus, Lois, I'm off 'ome.'

Keith buckling at the knees, sliding down the door.

'Bleddy 'ell, Lois, who'd 'ave kids today?'

'This is a little devil, Marjorie. Unlike his saintly father. Don't think any more about it. Join me in a strong cup of tea.'

'It's not you, Lois, it's yer children. I don't feel 'appy 'ere, not with they around me.'

"Please don't think any more of it. Come in the other room and eat a doughnut with me. To complement the pizza.'

The kitchen seemed a little spoiled by violence and memories restored, so they moved into the modern lounge, full of its outer-office furniture, the room which Lois disliked most of all. And I have known you, Marjorie, since we were kids ourselves, pumping up the bicycle tyres, leaving them in School Hill among the rocks and the thorn bushes, lying down on a bank behind a gorse bush; and somehow, I always scored every time and your chap talked about ferrets and looked out over the hillside where the cattle stood. And now, some of them are dead and some were slaughtered and some, like donkeys, go and come to their work. Despite my honeymoon, the blue striped wallpaper and the white panels with their little bumps picked out in gold paint, I am here, counting in my book of hours and what I am able to remember of them, with Marjorie, who cannot hear it. Tage out riding, in the missionary position, and my thinking, I wonder who else and how many have peeped out past these white shoulders. And all of that poisoned it until it lay in ruins all around me, and I could not go on, because I am too old and wary of anything to do with a man at all, expect little Davey, who at least knew his

12

business and was regular and consistent, and never lost his breath or anything else in the small hours of the upper rooms.

Marjorie talking, with no-one listening. The voice filtering through the panes and the golden privet, down the bank of weeds and on toward the pines in the valley churchyard, where the mist has drifted from the sea and settles on crusty tombstones which bear familiar names and lead us not into temptation.

CHAPTER 3

Another Saturday morning, the sun standing over the solemn acre of steel and concrete where couples walk, their fingers caught in wire baskets, after the soft intertwining of hands on Friday evening, which is now long, long ago. In the town, early trippers moving in the tide of traffic lights and pedestrian crossings. And in this chilly supermarket, quietly pushing the perambulator up the aisle to the checkout altar where a multitude stands and waits, like cows at milking time.

A warm, warm day, and the Swede is in my house, with his boots on my nineteenth century Persian rug, which can put up with anything and has withstood all the trampling of my slippered life, and that of generations before me, but which cannot tolerate the grit of cities, especially Swedish ones. And what I need is furniture from sales, the sort that feature on the middle pages of auction catalogues in black and white photographs, choice, distinguished, rare and comfortable. So that he would pack up the Scandinavian stuff designed by psychopaths and ship it back to the window where it belongs. And I don't see his mother's house full of that junk. Her furniture was imported from Kent and Vienna, the vases from Christie's. And the first night in that wretched bedroom full of doors, strutting around with no trousers, that thing dangling, which is far and away too large for a Scandinavian's, and you must have bad blood in you somewhere, old son, to have a thing that size, despite your nice blond curls. And was that what Marjorie was winking about when she said, 'Christ, Lois, you do always seem to land on yer feet.'

Teatime, Marjorie and Lois struggling up Toldhu Hill, with rolls of wallpaper and a pack of mirror tiles. Boys and girls draped over garden walls, pulling out soft brown stones, breaking them on the pavement. Mr Hicks from Liskeard, dumping three tons of paving slabs over camellias in a spotless garden, his mind on the bald patch over his forehead which he regards in the rear-view mirror; and the stones spread over the spotless bushes like excrement from the squatting lorry, while the wife from Leicester sobs and says that she doesn't know what a Delabole fireplace is and never wanted one on her lounge wall in the first place since gas is now available.

'We did right, moving over here, Marjorie.'

'Tha's Arthur 'Icks there, Lois.'

'Not bad on a fine day, this corner of the world.'

'An' some greet muscles on un. Used t' carry coal fer years 'til 'ee put 'is back out, and the doctors said 'ee'll never carry coal again, so 'ee went over the quarry to work.'

'Oh, for goodness sake, Marjorie.'

'Penaluna wasn' bad, y'knaw, before we got married. But I was daft an' went an' insisted upon it. We should 'a' stayed single, then 'ee might 'a' bin 'eaps different. All they Fridays we sat on the sofa, me sweepin' 'is 'hands off of me. When we got married, 'ee lost interest right away. I wasn' what they call a bad lookin' girl, neither. Now, I'm gone fat n' nobody do take a' interest.'

'Oh Marjorie, what a shame. Life is very cruel.'

'Naw. 'Tis the way things do go.'

Ah well. Saturday is the day when we go to town and empty our purses. We buy a lot of things to eat, and then we walk down to the town again and get a bit of wallpaper, a potted plant, a kitchen scales. A little lightness of spirit before the dark. In the evening, for some, dancing, or the public house.

'You know that sofa, Marjorie. The one you put in the garage last winter when you bought the new one. Can I have it? I'll pay you for it. Or I'll give you one of my Scandinavian tables. The nice glass one.'

'Cert'n'ly not.'

'The small table that swivels round, then.'

'Nope.'

'The drop leaf one.'

'I don' want yer tables.'

'Well, it's a deal, then.'

'Bleddy Hell, Lois, leave my sofa where 'tis, in the garage. I might need un one a these days. You got money, git an' buy one fer yerself. Y're always after my stuff. Why? You d' upset me sometimes.'

'Oh well, Marjorie, it's just that His sofa is new and I can get away with throwing it in the garage if I have to look after your old one first.'

'What do 'ee mean now? Don't be so damn silly.'

'Silly? Look ~ if I tell him this sofa is an ugly manifestation of his rigid little mind and, like him, it will have to go, he'll get selfish ideas in his big head. But if, in the kindness of my heart, I take in your sofa, which otherwise has to be put in an outhouse, not to say the garage or the *chy bychan*, then, it will only be a matter of time before he realises that your comfortable old sofa is where he wants to lie down. Then, he will throw out his own sofa, leaving me with the one I wanted in the first place. And he will say that he has a loving wife who is nice to her friends, even to the point of taking in their furniture. Strategy, my dear Marjorie.'

'So where do I come into this? I want my old sofa in my garage, where it do belong to be.'

'Why? It'll get mouldy out there, if it hasn't already.'

'It won't.'

'It will. And Penaluna can lock up his van at night again against the vandals. And the stars will shine down on a clear short drive up to your garage, and everything will be neat and pretty and you won't have to be ashamed or frightened when the Community Panda Car goes past Penaluna's vehicle and all will be harmony in Toldhu Close.'

'Well, I'll see. I'll discuss it with Penaluna.'

'You're a lovely woman, Marjorie.'

'You ought to 'ave gone on the stage.'

'Been everywhere else.'

Marjorie labouring up the hill, dropping the baskets in the roadway to haul up a shoulder strap. White bread will be the death of you, Mrs Penaluna. And so 'twill, so 'twill.

Lois swinging her bags into a cupboard in her garage and dodging out into the road again before the Swede stirs from Sports Special or the children come out, complaining that He's been brutalising them. Lolloping down the hill with her long legs, smoothing back her soft, boy's hair, beautifully cut and cleaned. In at this green and white teashop called The Green Apple, to meet someone equally sporting and special, this Sports Saturday.

'You look lovely, Lois.'

'Thankyou.'

'I'm sorry, but ~ is your husband in this country again?'

'Been in to the clinic, has he?'

'Oh Lois! Someone said he was here again. How do you feel about that?'

'It's very nice to welcome him here.'

'That's good.'

'I'll have to go soon.'

So you are curious about my awful life, young man. There is no need to be, for in a year or so, you'll be lying back on your own sofa, concerning yourself with football injuries which you will never have to treat, a grown man with your own little wife and television. So let it rest there.

Wandering across the rugby ground and down the river a little way, where we can see Malpas and the flat mud where one heron is standing, dipping into darkness. And the evening spreads out like that patient of Eliot's etherised upon the table, in this some-time forest where Tristan forded the river, seeking a place for him to love, in this small world.

Tristan takes my hand.

'Lois, may I kiss you?'

'I shouldn't think so.'

Walking along a little further towards the trees and the grasses, he speaks of his practical charity in foreign parts.

'There were twenty thousand refugees altogether ~ that's five large comprehensive schools.'

'Terrible to think of, on such a lovely evening at the beginning of summer.'

'Yes, this country is lovely. There were two small, government run camps. I completed some of my training there.'

'And now you are qualified. Look where the light falls upon the water.'

'Do you like walking? I used to walk in the evening, along the roads they have in the coffee estates, when it was cool.'

'Yes, I like walking.'

'Around Cornwall?'

'Just around here, with my pushchair and shopping baskets.'

'We used to cycle at school. Dozens of chaps cluttering up the lanes.'

'Yes. We went cycling too, my friend Marjorie and me, when we were at school. Will you stay in hospitals now, or will you go into general practice?'

'I'm interested in clinical work. But I don't know yet ~ not sure.'

'Really?'

'No.'

'And your tax position, working for too many hospitals at once?'

'I have an accountant.'

'All the more reason to be a GP, I should think. Then, somebody else can do your books, instead of you struggling with small cheques and declaring everything.'

Like me, for instance. After Davey's crafty fiddles and Tage's criminal evasions, this boy's books would hardly fulfil the summit of my creative talents in accounting. And what shall I tell him of my life and the begetting of my five horrid, wild, working-class children?

Ah, there are the trees, with their fresh leaves, limey soft, the beeches downy at this time of the year. And with age they toughen and polish themselves. Shall I talk to you, David John, of the red summer lofts in Sweden, the herds, the cow-bells, the point on the hillside where the trees give way to rocks and barren land which is like and utterly unlike our own?

And under the trees, the summer eve darkens into twilight, and we have timed it right, as the inner clock always does, so that we may rest here on the grass under the leaves if we want to. But I won't be lying down here this time, so that you will go back to your dwelling near the hospital and think what a wonderfully loyal woman, I must have her at any cost, no matter what Father or the Swede says, or the five brats at home. And oh, David John, after the age of twenty-five, nothing is new and everything is repetition. And anything you haven't learned yet, you never will. So, I am off home, back along the path which I know very well, and although you hold my hand and lead the way, it is I who know the pitfalls in the growing shade. Well, goodbye then, and perhaps I can see you next week or perhaps not. He may take me back to Flen with him, shut up my house and kick me back onto the boat, I really don't know, because although I will never say so, you will have to learn swiftly that your only hope of taking me is by storm or by stealth. Either will do.

David John standing on the pavement, hands in his sports jacket pockets, *desolé*. You have passed examinations, friend, but you haven't quite got the knack yet. Give me a man with along, fat one, who leaves me alone on the red days and loves me on demand and doesn't go in at the tradesmen's entrance when I am suffering from the piles after yet another birth. And I am beginning to forget the younger children's names.

Enter the house quietly and stand in the tiny hall. No sounds of children and none of Tage. Must be asleep in front of Match of the Day. Don't think he knows much about the game, and certainly doesn't know my score. I don't have an alibi, so where have I been all day? Not with Marjorie. She will have been here already this evening, raising her eyebrows. 'But I left Lois yer, just outside th'house, with 'er shoppin'. 'Twas jes gone four.' No, I definitely haven't been with Marjorie. Marjorie will be the death of me. Best story is the market and then the gardening centre, which stays open until ten. But I haven't got any plants. Ah well then I'll have to sneak out tomorrow morning and order a fishpond on the public telephone which they'd better deliver quick. And why the hell do I ever bother? I just hope they stock fishponds. It would be like them not to. Very difficult to keep a little excitement going, with Tage in this house. Never should have married the swine and now I can't see young David John when I want to, which will cost me in the end. Just when things are getting to a pitch. Much rather be a doctor's wife than a Swedish farmer's wife. I bet I'm not entitled to any widow's pension if he dies first. Damn foreigners. This isn't for me, this marriage business. And family doctors' wives live well in large houses with rose gardens and small stone lions at both sides of the door. And a fishpond is a small if unnecessary investment at times like these, when I have a feeling I'm in deep water, coming home so late, having been nowhere all day. Perhaps I just got sick in the head, had a depression and took the bus to Perranporth to drown myself, changed my mind and got the last bus back. Much more feasible. Any Swede would swallow that. Marjorie's right. I should have gone on the stage. With a talent like mine.

Lois, kicking off her muddy shoes, going softly up the stairs, checking her face in the long mirror of the wardrobe. Such a pink and white, eye-catching face.

'Cornish, Celtic bitch.'

Oh dear, not as one hoped. Heavy footsteps on the carpet, which tell of canned lager and fourteen nil.

Slipping the sewing scissors into her cardigan pocket by way of defence.

Tage downstairs slamming his fist into his palm. The net curtain blowing gently by the open window, Lois slipping between the sheets fully clothed, the bedroom door locked. Waking up hot, the stars winking outside. Bleary silence in the house of forgotten Saturday anger. Lois creeping into the bathroom. The cystitis will be the death of me. And no-one knows why or how or what the cure might be, except bicarbonate of soda, which works for a short while, but only for decent women. And, like the idiot I am, I've always made the mistake of pulling the flush.

And the Swede reaching the top of the stairs in three or four leaps, driving his wife back into the bathroom, knocking a scream out of her before it begins. Dragging Lois across the landing, her toes pulling up the carpet and catching the wooden posts of the banister. Lois opening first the left eye, the not so good one, and then the right eye, the perfect one; and neither of them damaged, my gold tooth in its place in my mouth, which doesn't hurt either. And all round, seeming intact, if sore under the ribs but sick in the guts. A curious thing, this anatomy because, of all things, it is the conscience which should hurt the most. Or so they tell me.

CHAPTER 4

Someone was tapping her shoulder. Turning over in the bed to find the Swede leaning on an elbow, smiling somewhat affectionately, though not entirely so.

'How are you? Had enough? How are you today? Would you like some of my coffee? Where you were, all of yesterday? Why you don't answer to me? What is the matter? Do you care about your little children?'

'Sorry, Tage, what was the question? My hearing is gone. You will have to speak up.'

'Where you were yesterday, Lois? What did you yesterday?'

Lois, hunting for the telephone, first in the bedside cabinet, then under the bed.

'I'll make a statement to the solicitor, shall I? When I find the telephone.'

'Oh my God. What a wife this is. To have a wife like this. And I thought I was so lucky. But you are a dog, after all I have done. Why did I marry?'

'You're still sleeping, Tage.'

'I am not sleeping. I have not slept all night. Where have you been yesterday? What have you been doing in town? The children said always you do this.'

'The children said you always do this. Reported speech, accusative.'

'The children say you always do this. So. It makes no difference. You always do this. The children say it. From the teeth, tongue of children.'

'Mouth of babes, out of the.'

'You are a dog. Where have you go? The baby, he was howl all day. I telephone to Marjorie. She said change him. But first I change you.'

'Oh good old Marj, always first with the ideas.'

'Lois, where did you gone? Marjorie had leave you at four o'clock outside this house. She told to me.'

'I go to sleep, Tage. Yes?'

'Did you see a man?'

'Yes of course. I see men everywhere. I think I see a man in this bed. Get out of it and go in the kitchen.'

'Ah ~ so you saw a man. I think so. This is the truth. You saw a man. You are a bad woman.'

'Keep talking, Tage.'

'Keep talking. You are a bad woman.'

Tage slamming his fist into his hand in that very annoying manner when one wanted to doze in the evening and the morning, after a tense, hot night. His grammar slips when he is being silly. And all this fuss after one slides home pure and unsullied from the doctor's. When one thinks, love, love. Not so much fighting. Reaching up with the right hand to tug softly at the small hairs at the nape of the neck, and what is a man good for, anyway? Scratching at his shoulder with the gentle tip of the fingernails, watching the modulating mood, the light coming back into the slate grey eyes.

In my softest contralto, *adagio*, 'I saw the doctor in town, and went to the Garden Centre. I have a surprise. A fishpond. And I am sick all the time. I've caught it again. So don't hit me any more.'

No effect. He doesn't understand one's euphemisms, not as the blood understands in the surge and flow in that thing under the fingers of my left hand. Languid, reaching with my right for the scissors in the cardigan pocket, thumb and finger opening them out. Slam my backside down on this chest. Insert a scissor just under the foreskin and take the tiniest of snips. And the husband, he howl all the day. But sadly, I am not big like Marjorie, and what is the value of intent without the authority of her fifteen stones?

Lois walked down to the newsagent's with the baby in the pushchair. Stood by a tree in the park where she often went to clear her mind. Over there, the river. Over there, the houses slipping down the hillside, inch by uneven inch, where she must live for a while longer, until her luck changed. If it ever did. Tage was a waste of time. And ate too much. And had no dress sense. A very vulgar man. The short answer was divorce. And then? Listen to the wind in the trees, the wind howl, long after the baby stops its howling and grows into a man, long after I am gone and my brood are scattered. And there will always be the howling of babes, and the tight mouths of battered women who struggle to make something of existence, long after my name has disappeared from all registers.

Next? A cream cake, a tub of ice-cream, a piece of fruit, cram it into him and listen to what eternity has to say to me. Know your enemy. And then pick him off. Organ by organ. An eye for an eye. Always criticising me and telling me to hold in my stomach, as though I was sixteen and the children were gestated in a nest. Clean my nails, have my teeth capped, get my shoes repaired. As though I am poor, and not up to scratch.

All the rooftops steaming after hard rain. How I love the summer. Took Marjorie into that hospital over there to have a wart cut off. 'It interferes with her . . . life, doctor.' 'Yes, I can see that. Must be a pain in the arse to have a wart there, Mrs Penaluna.' Polite laughter from the students, who have heard that one before. A little freezing of the hind quarters, a knot tied, to stop the blood, and off it drops within a week. Satisfaction guaranteed, and nothing to pay. Wash the hands and step into the sportscar.

The Registry Office, hidden behind the clock which conceals the public lavatory. Lois, going out of her way to stay close to Facilities. Sometimes I think the cystitis will eat me alive. And it was in that dreadful place that Mary was married to some miner or other called Roger Lett, and they had an argument in front of the Registrar because Mary thought he was called Mee, but he was really called Lett. And he told her that people only called him Me because of Lett: 'let me, a joke, see?' But Mary wasn't having any name like that and was ready to call it off, and would have done, but for her condition. And those were the days before the abortion industry, which must have changed the course of Protestant history. All those strong boys and pretty maids chopped up and flushed out. And it always seemed to Shakespeare and me that illegitimacy bred the lions of England, and the stale marriage bed the asthma and milk rash. It must have been all of fifteen years ago, but it seems like yesterday, with the registrar demanding the money first and isn't anybody else coming? Just me in my headscarf and Mary's mother, with my little Joseph in the pram. A religious occasion. They don't make marriages like that any more. Everything is planned these days.

Into the doctor's, with its wooden benches and uniformed ladies taking themselves seriously. Through the hatch with the spice bottle of urine which bears its label, Pure Saffron Stamens, and that may explain why this looks like chronic nephritis and leprosy.

Twenty other women on the wooden benches.

'Hello Lois.'

'Oh hello, you two. Didn't know you came here.'

'Have to.'

'Still on the sick, then?'

'Oh yes.'

Lazy devils. They've been on and off work since I left the canteen. What a good job that was, until Davey stuck his oar in, and I couldn't fry eggs without vomiting. That vicious supervisor, Manhire. 'Can't do without you frying the eggs,

Lois.' And the custard tank that was never drained. Ought to have been prosecuted, that lot.

An angel in white at the hatch.

'Do you wish to see the doctor today, Mrs Af Klercker?'

'No, I won't today. Just don't mix up my pee with the invalids'.' Lois pointing her finger with a grimace.

'Oh, Mrs Af Klercker, we never do that.'

One day, I'll ask whether this is where they change the water into Watneys. But not today. Today is a moment in which to pause, between a body left to itself, its old injuries, its sticky bits of scar tissue, its attempts at variations, its warts and delinquent growths, and between the minute when they tell you, peering through the hatch, 'Which card is it . . . oh yes,' you're definitely up there without a paddle again and we're sorry, Mrs Af Klercker. Have it stitched up next time. No bother these days. On the contrary, dear ladies, a white nursery with daffodil curtains, soft silk yellow walls and plenty to eat and drink is all I require now. And wouldn't that suit Marjorie too, and God knows, Marjorie, there are plenty of men barking after you, but you have to get out there, with your first class intelligence and your white high heels. Penaluna's van doesn't run you up to Heaven.

'Good afternoon, Mrs Af Klercker.'

'Cheerio Lois.'

Goodbye, dear ladies, goodbye.

And drawing into the post office with the pushchair. The bounty of family allowance. Shake out the yellow book. Here is my reward. A fine system, which has saved us all, one way and another, and has made a drone out of men.

Past Fagash Lil, who sits on the green chair, placed just so for the benefit of the public, but not for types like Lil. Standing at the double-glazed, sound-proof grille, a seedy young grammar-school Janner counting his slips of paper as though they were gold leaf. A picture of some farmhouse kitchen I have never seen comes into my mind, apropos of nothing. The mind keeps doing this. I can smell the cattleshed, which is very close to the open door. Is money nothing other than happiness delayed?

'My family allowance book.'

'Mrs Af Klercker?'

'Yes yes yes yes.'

'Is your husband living with you at present? I thought I saw him with you in the park this week. We live in Mabaley Crescent. You can't have the additional allowance if he lives with you.'

Not I, this lady accompanist in the park this week.

'Of course I am not living with him, nor he with me, and the woman in the park will have a lot to answer for. Give me your name. I will need you as a witness.'

'Sorry, Mrs Af Klercker, I understand he is living with you. I saw him come out of the house myself. You have been reported several times, and as it says in the back of your book section ten, one must report and return the order book or books to your local security office without cashing any further orders if, A, you begin to live with someone as man and wife, marry, re-marry, become reconciled or resume residing with your spouse. Surely you now come under section A, Mrs Af Klercker.'

A dangerous look on Lois' face. The man retreats further behind his wire netting.

'Af Klercker was indeed here. He divided the Swedish furniture in half with my axe. He has attacked my wooden leg, but fortune has smiled upon me. My English oak leg was provided by our National Health Service. I am an invalid, a cripple, pregnant and utterly, utterly alone in this world. Regrettably I am not also a black foreigner, but with my considerable disabilities, I should fulfil most requirements, don't you think? I would advise you to stay in Moberley

Crescent, friend, and not to spy informally upon the innocent and suffering. My family allowance, if you please. My latest affliction makes me short of breath or I would tweak your ear, you little git.'

Money counted out, white lips and dark glares all around, the public line shuffling its feet. Lois outside, pausing by a pillar, trembling a little. Upsets and breathlessness are to be avoided now, on this, a day of many hard days. The dark, cold granite of these pavements; and underneath, the deadly radon gases of the underworld. My mining and farming family. Generations who died young; Davey and me making up for it all in our blind solitude, reaching out across the white claywashed moor of the kitchen under Tregajorran Hill. Five boys, our part in the battle against the interloper. And they will all be cut down like the Sunday daisies on Penaluna's lawn, come the Sabbath. I must eat something or be sick.

This watery cafe with its traders from the Flea Market. Takes me back to real market days, with guarded talk about subsidies and planning permissions. And you up-country fly-by-nights will be off when the going gets rough. We will be left to our own.

Count the money and tuck it away. A day of spending. A refill for the gas fire, a look in the second-hand shop for a baby's cot, though I shan't need it yet. This tarted up granite town which makes me cry. Snapping away at buildings with the tiny Kodak which belongs to my son. And as these steep-roofed, galvanised iron monuments fall, what will it mean to us, sneaking a snap here and there of the rat-run quayside ruins? County Councillors barking, brightly lit receptions, the power of a single thought, a little whisper, tongue on teeth, the oscillating bridge of an idea, the rising tide of decision.

Let us go then, you and I, and snap away as they pull down even City Hall itself.

CHAPTER 5

And now, it was almost summer. In the Memorial Park, the early retired wandered about with their dogs, watching out for layabout teenagers and the jobless unemployed. Voters with opinions, the poor opinionated hanging on for revenge at the ballot box. It was almost summer and Lois laboured up the hillside, smiling at the nice primroses, the calves of her legs easing as she turned down the curve of Toldhu Crescent into Marjorie's back garden at number seven, 'Ennisfree'. Free of Ennis, the landlord of the two basement rooms where Penaluna and Marjorie had begun married life fourteen years before their entry into this paradise on the hill; Penaluna, in a rare burst of homely enthusiasm, had bent a yard of shining steel wire into the house name of his choice. And what meaning and significance it had for him. Much more significance than that poetic name carved in hardwood next door: 'Stoney Broke.' What a silly name.

There she was ~ Marjorie boiling a kettle, an eye on a fresh pimple under the upper arm, pulling the white flesh towards her, wondering what was going wrong.

'Oh Lois.'

Marjorie opened the door and Lois walked in. An untidy kitchen with a strong sense of Penaluna in it. A pair of his shoes in the corner, beside a tin of shoe polish and a rag; his stockings pushed into the heels, so as not to be lost or forgotten or put into the wash too soon.

'Spring cleaning, Marjorie? Lots to do? Darning, mending, cooking, fencing?'

'Is the kitchen dirty? We'll go out. You don't have to stay 'ere.'

'Aren't you spring cleaning this year? You usually do.'

'Nope. I aren't spring cleanin' this year. I aren't spendin' a farthin' on paint. I'm leaving Cornwall.'

'What?'

'I'm leavin' Cornwall. Givin' up, gwoin up country. I'm a free woman an' I got no children.'

'Where? Where are you going?'

'London. Where everybody do go except me.'

'Well . . . to do what?'

'I dunno. I'll find out when I do get there. I never bin nowhere in my life . . . not even Paddin'ton Station.'

'But it's big and ugly and dangerous and without a job . . .'

'I'm gwoin tomorrow morn' early, before Penaluna gits up. I got a bag full of clothes an' my 'ousekeepin' money in the washin' machine. My pink suit is in the wardrobe all ready. I got a new pair of tights an' I shall wear my white shoes. I know they'll git dirty in the train, but I do like them. I'll take me white handbag as well, an' I know you'll say the black one is better. I know I shall look like I'm gwoin to a weddin' accordin' to you, and I'll never git a job in a pink crimpolene suit. Well, I don't give a damn. Tha's the way I'm gwoin, an' I don't give a damn. I don't want no comments, arguments nor suggestions, neither.'

'Well done, Marjorie.'

'Eh? Yes, well.'

Lois looking around the kitchen.

'What about the house, keeping it clean . . . Penaluna and all that . . . your life's work?'

Marjorie turning off the kettle.

'Finished.'

'What about that new coffee machine you had for your anniversary? You haven't taken it out of the box. It still has the instructions and guarantee on it.'

'Take it. You know 'ow to use things like that. I don't. I got married a 'undred an' twenty years back an' it 'as seemed like 'ell. I got no children an' no life. I got to live with old furniture that Penaluna do put in 'ere. I got carpets that aren't paid for. My bedroom is full of junk an' I got one cardboard box of me own under the bed, full of nonsense I stopped addin' to when I was eighteen, so I'm gwoin to London in me white shoes because tha's where I left off, as far as I am concerned.'

'In a pink suit and white shoes.'

'Yeah, so there you are. You can 'ave the anniversary coffee machine. I know you do envy me un. I'm gone to London to seek me ruin at last. Penaluna'll go mad. I don't care, though. Not no more. I 'ave every right.'

'Well . . . what is it Marjorie? What went wrong?'

'Wrong? Nothin' went wrong. I got sicker and sicker and then one day I got better.'

'Alright.'

'Come on . . . take yer coffee machine before I do git sentimental. I was never meant to 'ave nothin'. Shan't be needin' it where I'm gwoin. I'll never come back 'ere. An' one day I'll 'ave a dozen coffee machines. I been too petty . . . tha's my downfall. Too stupid, too quiet. I paid too much for my little luxuries in life. A place to sleep, a sofa to sit on. I wasted it all.'

'What about the blender?'

'Take that as well. Take it. I shan't be blendin' from now on.'

Lois fixed the lid down tightly. For the next baby. Lovely fresh food for him, all pulverised and digestible in an instant. Poor baby. Poor Marjorie. One could weep for Marjorie, who had a good food mixer as well.

'This food mixer, Marjorie.'

'Make a good dough an' good shortcrust pastry for pasties. My youth is etched in the bottom of the bowl there.'

'Penaluna doesn't want it?'

'Why not? It's 'is, alright.'

'He'd sell it.'

'I know 'ee will. 'Ee'll never find another poor woman to keep it gwoin for'n, anyhow, not like I done all these years.'

Lois, staring at the food mixer, a worn food mixer with old-fashioned dials.

'He'll sell it. He'll advertise it in the paper, and when he can't sell it for enough, he'll take it down to the auctions. Or down to the market for a few pence. He'll get rid of it . . . all your labour all these years. And buy his pasties in the shop. He'll eradicate all traces of you in the end.'

'Oh shut up. If you do want un, take un. Don't make it worse for me. It's easy for me to go . . . but not that easy. I'm still a bit sentimental, like.'

The two of them leaving the house. Locking the door, sauntering through the Crescent in the sunlight. This is our heritage and all we shall have of it. Robbed blind since the cradle . . . and there was no cradle, come to think of it, only a second-hand perambulator from Social Services which, later, served for the cat and generations of drowned kittens. This is no paradise, nor any improvement, and the landlord's face is not seen around these parts. Only the bankrupt builder. We do not know who we must blame for these, our trials.

Down the tarmacadamed hill in silence, Lois displaced, empty inside, with no longing, even for a change, just a brief understanding, a small insight. Marjorie a step or two behind, with none of the same small comprehension.

'I'm glad I never 'ad no children now. You are tied 'and an' foot, Lois, you'll never get out until they are all growed, an' then it will be too late. You'll be stuck with yer teapot and the National Housewives' Register for laughs. Pathetic.'

'Don't be so cruel. Everything changes, Marjorie. Nothing is like even this forever.'

'I can't see that.'

'I was a teacher once; and before that, a proper smallholder's wife.'

'All the same thing. Toldhu Close, like I said, Toldhu Close is the 'igh spot in your life. After this . . . nothin'. Everythin' you done before was a preparation for the 'ights. We'll 'ave a cup of tea in town, shall us? Are you goin' to buy anythin'?'

Lois putting Marjorie's choice electrical goods in her garage, on the way to town again.

'Glad I'm leavin', eh?'

'No, Marjorie, just concerned for your things.'

'You 'aven't said good luck 'r any of the things good friends do say to each other.'

'Good luck . . . but if you don't have luck, you'll die. So, good luck isn't strong enough, old friend.'

'Thanks any'ow, Lois.'

That uneasy walk to town, the last they would make together, a definable sense of betrayal and desertion between them, two old friends. Here, the Green Apple, more subdued than on Saturdays.

'Lookin' forward to tomorrow. 'Aven't bin on a train fer years. It used to be coaches an' outin's to Plymouth. Might be some interestin' man on the train, to while away the time.'

'I doubt it, Marjorie.'

'Yeah, if I could find a man on the train runnin' away too . . . that would be a 'elp. A nice chap with brains an' somethin' to say. Like a 'lectrician or a . . . well, they don't run away. But, you know, somebody startin' out again, like me, with their own car. Somebody with a job. Old Penaluna never 'ad a job, you know. Always grubbin' aroun' with second-'and stuff. I got fed up with it, never knowin' what money was comin' in.'

'Marjorie, you're trying to get away from one man, now you're looking for another.'

Two other women sitting together in a corner, drinking tea.

'What shall us 'ave, Lois?'

'The ethnic drink, Marjorie. Despite all assurances, it will be stewed and I shall be ill.'

'You could 'ave 'ot chocolate, seein' it's my last day an' this is the last time we shall be together.'

'I wouldn't bet on it, old friend.'

Lois never forgetting her own goodbyes to familiar habits, her exits and entrances in the only place she knows, where it is possible to be oneself, is it? No, not at all. Not at all. Like a page of Ceefax, insubstantial, hardly recallable, a sheet of information, altering by the day, Lois' small life. By middle age, one could discount discovery or intention, let alone invention.

'Just the rest of today an' I'm off. Off to London, that terrible place. I'll git a job of me own an' a flat. An' you can come an' stay with me when Tage is 'ere with yer kids.'

'He'll wall them up in the garage, Marjorie.'

'They're nice kids you got, Lois, I don't say they aren't, an' I don't say they're not worth settlin' down for . . . but me, I never bin nowhere. I settled down afore I even knowed it. I 'ad nothin' to do all day that was worth doin'. After the farmin' you 'ad a intelligent life, as you do call it, but I 'ad no life. Penaluna is no beast, but 'ow would I know if he was? I've 'ad no experience, nothin' to compare 'im with. Sometimes I do feel sick in the kitchen, thinkin' about what I 'ave missed.'

'Oh poor Marjorie. Raw experience doesn't mean anything.'

'A great day, this. A great new opportunity. A final burst out of the net. The way it should be. The way it really should be, Lois. They'll be fightin' over me, the way you said they would, years ago. What chance 'ave I 'ad before this?'

'Chances are always there, every hour. It's recognising the ones that matter, that have some significance, that's the art of it. You shouldn't take just anything. I never meant that.'

'Where did I go wrong before, Lois?'

'You were a nice, big woman, Marjorie, who played by the rules as you should. Nobody can be asked to do that forever. Eventually . . .'

'I bin decent all my life, shame upon me. Mind you, I think Penaluna 'as as well. But who can say? Nobody would tell us, Lois. Per'aps they would. Depends who they are. I don't know what Penaluna do git up to on a Friday. Every Friday since I was seventeen, 'ee's bin gwoin' out on 'is own. With the boys, he do say. Well, they boys are growed up an' gone, playin' bingo with their missus an' takin' the kids to discos on a Friday, an' 'ee's still gwoin' out with them every Friday, so 'ee do say. Who does 'ee think 'ee's talking' to? I do know 'ee 'as a woman, because 'ee do never miss, not even when 'is mother died. Good luck t'n, any'ow, I don't resent it, not now. I did resent it, long enough, but tha's all swept clean now. I'm out of it. I complained an' competed too long. She can come out a the woodwork now, poor soul, whoever she is. She's bin there long enough. I was no competition, for sure. Like you said before, the minute you give everythin' up, you git everythin', an' you don't want it no more.'

'I wasn't thinking about that at the time, Marjorie. But look, have you got enough money?'

Marjorie sitting upright. Lifting the teacup.

'Have you really enough money, Marjorie? Do you know what it costs to live in London, just to find a room . . . even if you last that long up there?'

Marjorie got up, moving the table forward with a scraping sound, all stomach and knees.

'I'm gettin' out of 'ere before you do try an' ruin my confidence in meself again.'

Marjorie moving to the door, idle pairs of eyes upon her, a striking woman in white shoes, who, dressed differently, could have been a provincial mayoress, even a lady author.

Slight little Lois, aware of the sad irony of Marjorie's floating charm.

'Marjorie, I've a hundred quid in my bag. Take it with you. Not to spend. Just in case. Don't go to the big city without money. It's fatal. Or could be. At your time of life. Come on, Marjorie, I'm not giving it to you. You may need more than you think.'

'No. Too kind of 'ee.'

'It's not kindness.'

'What is it, then? You think I can't survive all by myself. Think I'll be back in a week, all the leather worn off me shoes? Think I can't speak enough English to find a room an' a job? Think I can't keep clean without my bath an' my big 'andbasin? Come on, Lois, I watch television. I know what's gwoin on in the worl'. I've 'eard all about the big city. There's nothin' to protect me from.'

They stood face to face outside the cafe, customers watching them from behind plate glass. Lois, reaching into her handbag, thrusting banknote after banknote into her friend's hands. To the amazement of all. Marjorie with her mouth wide open. Lois determined, her little mouth shut down.

'Alright, Marjorie. That's your emergency cash. Now I feel happier about you going. Not much, but a bit. Don't let me down. I don't know how you could do this, anyway.'

'I don't know either, Lois.'

'Oh go on, Marjorie, ruin yourself at last. It can't matter any more now, to you, to me, to anybody, if it comes to that. There's something else, though: I want my money back with interest.'

'Oh Lois, I don't know what to say.'

'I say that for myself, Marjorie. Like the enlightened Christian.'

'The joy of givin'.'

'I want it back. As a reward for my sacrifice. I shall need it again. I need it now. With all my children. I can't go to work. There is no work, and I can't work. I have to rely on Tage. It's a terrible thing. What can I do?'

'I don't know.'

'I'll tell you something.'

Lois, catching hold of Marjorie's forearm, walking her along the pavement, away from the eyes of the sippers behind the plate glass.

'Something I never told you.'

'Carry on.'

'This is it, Marjorie. Don't listen to anything I say to you. I've had it. In life. I've had it and done it all. I've gone on producing children to spite myself. The way some people bite their nails. It's a kind of anger. You don't know. You don't understand. You are still a girl, Marjorie, and for all your size and age, vulnerable, like a big schoolgirl. Yes. I feel for you, as a mother does. You don't know anything yet. And perhaps you never will. This is one life, the West Briton and the pot of tea, the net curtains at the window, which we all live and complain about. And look, there is another, which is England . . . or in my case, Sweden. And up there in London, you are on your own, absolutely . . . orphaned. Like it was at school when Stink Hendy ordered you out in front of the class to solve the equation, and you couldn't do anything towards it because instead of listening to the lessons, you'd spent weeks staring at the clouds through Silas Trevail's gothic windows, thinking how it was going to be when the boat finally came in. I'll say no more. I'm not getting through.'

Marjorie scratched her head. The hair was coming out. The roots were too far apart.

'I don't know what to say to 'ee, Lois. I'm 'opeless when it do come to explainin' meself. I'm lackin' all confidence again, Lois, I wish I 'ad gone without tellin' 'ee. Are 'ee doin' it on purpose to me? Like a mother, spoilin' me fun.'

Marjorie perplexed, Lois filling up with melancholy. The detritus of women's lives. Merits no discussion. 'The joy of woman is the death of her most best beloved . . .'

'I find it most difficult to speak about things which, when it comes to it, really ought to be left unsaid. Those things which pass between men and women, generation to generation, they are not for discussion, even between old friends like us. Only for rediscovery. As are all things pertaining to real life. If man as a species would learn wisdom by accumulation of knowledge . . . as he had done in technology . . . but why go off on that track? I am no feminist, far from it. It so happened, I have produced nothing but boys, and they wear me into the ground. I don't understand them any more than I understood their father. But if I had a daughter, I would say this to her: promiscuity leads to disease and infertility. There is no cure for either, and sterility, whatever the cause, is an admission to Hell. Our lives are all about the shedding of blood, hence the complicated nature of things. Enclosed in the body, one lives, as much as one can. None of us should be afraid of life. But living: there is an art. Remember only this, this only: nature, like the National Health, is no respecter of age. It was a revelation which came to me at the age of seventeen, when my teeth first fought it out with an iron radiator in the hospital. Paul was born eventually, after twenty hours of such revelations, when I had already seen that my life was a second-class absurdity, and it had only just begun.'

'Lois, you are so gloomy. Whatever happened in the hospital that time?'

'Oh my. You miss the point. I tell you ~ the individual, the mother, we are an instrument of nature, nothing more. Some blame it all on men, but that is foolish. They are universally irrelevant in all this. You don't know, Marjorie. That's all I'm saying. And no-one can tell you. No-one can live life for you. Go and see. Go and see, little one. I won't be there to help you in Notting Hill or Chalk Farm or some other gutter. But here's a coin for the telephone, if you can find a good one, and I will be there, at the other end, waiting with advice to come back home. They all come home, with sickening regularity. Tell me one who hasn't. The infant in the cradle, the *ingrate* who lets nobody sleep. Between Davey, the blood, the babies sucking, I felt thoroughly done over. Insignificant to the point of invisibility. Sex, Marjorie, the wasted art of nothing heaped upon nothing. Anybody can do that. It is the commitment, the absence of the birth pill, the awe of another moment of impending, disastrous pregnancy. That is life, the knowledge of which flashes momentarily between the man and the woman. Choose a man under those conditions and you won't choose lightly or change your mind and swop about too soon. But he will. And so you take your small opportunity in life. But you don't have very long. Without it, you will have no life at all. Some choose not to dabble with these things at all. I think that's better, and attracts a lot of sympathy, if not honour.'

'Nobody could call you dull, Lois.'

'I don't ask for fun, and I don't ask for life to be worn away so fast. Not by my children, my bastards. Stay out of it, Marjorie. Don't make any comment. You are wide of the mark. After life with Davey was over, I raised my head from the eternal infant sucking, I too thought I would see what was out there. There was nothing good out there, of course. A wasteland of paper and empty classrooms filling up with the abandoned, the divorced, the hopeful, and worse. Even the demands upon a mother do not equal those furious demands made upon a language teacher. To exchange a bib full of wet rusk and a teatowel which has mopped up spilled tea for a polished table and napkins ~ the effort involved in changing the symbol for one's understanding of life is not worth the effort. Well, you don't understand, and you won't, not until everything is gone that you know, of me and of Penaluna and of Toldhu Estate. Why should you be gifted with the prior knowledge? And if you can make it to the coinbox telephone, from the gutter or from the polished table with the napkins ~ doesn't matter which ~ if you can remember even your old address, I should be surprised ~ very surprised ~ because life is like that. The most solid of things become a mirage in a short time. All this you should be able to see for yourself.'

'A nice tale, Lois. I don't know what to make of un, nor what you do mean by un.'

They crossed the street, and Marjorie bought a Woman's Realm, Lois shaking her head, making no comment, her outburst lost on her old friend. They looked an ordinary enough pair, one fat, one thin, middle-aged women; one a dreamer, one with a hard face, both Cornishwomen.

'What I like about Cornwall is this. You know who hates you. All I want in life is a beautiful house, plenty of money, a hobby or two, the children grown up, no more struggle. But there's always something ~ broken chairs, smashed crockery, faded curtains, bad health, the piles. Too many children, the wrong furniture, the right house in the wrong place. The wrong house in the right place. A sickening destiny of which we have some prescience. When everything goes right, you fear it going wrong. And of course it will go wrong. You have a good, happy life and you fear his infidelity, about which you are probably quite right. All these people who pass by here are in the same fix.'

'You're not like that, Lois.'

'You, Marjorie, are a terrible dreamer. You think you have nothing and there is nothing to lose. That's just it. In Penaluna you have everything you will ever get, and you don't know what it is you have to lose. But if you want to find out, then find out. You'll never be the same again.'

'Thank God for that, dear.'

'Oh well, keep in touch. You'll be alright. I just hope Penaluna doesn't have any woman out there on the doorstep, waiting like the cat. They usually do. You will need to go back, even as a new woman. I can tell you that much.'

At the Cathedral, Lois turned away, taking a leaflet from a boy with a placard proclaiming cheap jewels.

'Alright, I'm off now. I won't say goodbye. The world is round. We shall meet again.'

'Thanks again, Lois. Thanks for the money, tha's fine, thanks for everythin', for the advice.'

'Just make your fortune and give it back to me. Goodbye. I've had enough.'

'Goodbye.'

'Alright then.'

'Take care of yerself, Lois.'

'No, you take care, Marjorie. This is serious. Nothing will be the same.'

Marjorie stood on her best leg, a small hand on a massive hip, handbag over her arm. Lois, sad, full of sorrow, wary of the present, sorrowful of sorrows to come, which nobody knew of yet. Not her best friend.

41

Marjorie Penaluna, 'the head of the moon', as Penaluna called himself during that fanciful honeymoon phase of life, a pleasant enough surname. 'The head of a lunatic', a more appropriate derivation, one of his customers said later. Proud and ready now, ready for anything. Off to the big one, with twenty thousand Cornishwomen. To find the reason why not. To be English, with a job and money, and no Penaluna to drag her down.

CHAPTER 6

Summer, summer. Nothing to think about. Blue, high sky, like the skies of south China. Switch off the electric. The gas fire can rust now.

The milkman called, two weeks ago. In a dreadful state at seven in the morning. Some woman had propositioned him, his wife in the hospital with the new baby. Nothing to be upset about. All milkmen had the same to put up with. It happened to Penaluna once, over a second-hand cooker, which he was delivering. But they say he had the best of the bargain that time.

Tage Af Klercker still in Cornwall, altering the garden, painting the windows green, horrid budgie green, to keep out the wet. But paint only makes unseasoned wood worse.

Better to be in Flen, my son. Blue and white farmhouse windows, nice broad windows. Very nice. Not like here . . . damp green moulds, uncertain, nasty, deceptive climate, a tourist industry that ruins everything. Mining industry that leaves stopes under the living room, caverns measureless to man and surveyor under the garage. Here, a coal lorry passes a mile away, and you hear it chug under the kitchen floor.

This new house, though, was built on fields. Fields of the enclosures. Not on reclaimed fields. There is a difference. We both love the new house. The kids think it's marvellous to be close to town and have friends to play with in the evenings. They mix with nice boys on the estate and don't get into trouble. The police rambles are favourite pastimes here. They go at a pace which suits our boys, but they don't go anymore, not since small change and credit cards went missing. Sport is the thing these days, with young boys. They like football in season and cricket in the other season. Very organised, these English seasons. There is open season and closed season for teaching and teachers too. The schools are nearby, and all the children walk to the school bus, which is as well for Lois, who has her work cut out, with the next one coming along and the youngest only just started to crawl.

The living-room had been painted in this year's beige, to keep up with the times. There are two sofas in the living-room, which do not match in an interesting sort of way. One belongs to Marjorie. Lois can't decide which one has to go, but it won't be Marjorie's. One side of the tiny bathroom is covered with mirror tiles, rather beautifully well fixed. Tiles are possible because the walls in the bathroom are upright and correct. Tage spring-cleaned the house this year. It was his idea. Lois would never have asked him. She would wait. And her boys would never dream of helping. They think they are going back to their father and their farm as soon as they leave school.

The butcher comes twice a week. Lois has a freezer full of meat in the garage, and she eats little of that, but the butcher is a comfort, a routine, and gets upset when she tries to cut down the amount she buys from him. In the old style, she takes her plate out to the van, as her mother used to do, so very very long ago. It seems. The small ritual is a tradition, and in these uncertain times, in this unfamiliar place, we cling to tradition. What else do we have? He charges too much, of course. Every van man charges too much, including Penaluna, who comes around with vegetables, televisions, computers and God knows what else. Still, the faces at the open van doors say something to Lois, something soothing and contented in this tense world of decorating and making ready. Neighbours giggle, some of them. Lois is showing again, in her special tunic for these occasions. Tage is looking smug, and has bought a walking stick. Now, they go out together, arm in arm, walking in the park, where people like them very much and say good evening to them.

These months ahead, facing them as a series, as a collection of unspent days. That is the way. No drinking in the public house, no late nights, no sudden flare-ups and tempers, no arguments. No looking at the other men. Not much interest in anything now. My old friend Marjorie has gone, and I miss her. She hammered in so many missing pieces and created so many others with her circular saw in this jigsaw life. No sign of her. Perhaps she made it after all. So far so good.

I made a little dress for the baby, in case it is at last the little girl I always wanted, and as usual, there is a sense of unreality about it all, despite the signs. But it will come. Like a season. Like everything else present in this predictable land. Because, never doubt it, we have a destiny which we cannot deny or escape. I believe that. And always will. And all the thinking which I do here, dangling my legs over the side of the bed in the long afternoon, with Woman's Hour as a leit motif, confirms me in my opinion and prejudice.

In the first morning light, I make cups of tea. Four o'clock. Twelve hours early or late, the kettle boils. Last year's baby smiles and rolls over like a bridegroom, fast asleep on the kitchen floor, where I have changed the wet suit for a dry one. All is well, but for my horde upstairs, who invade even my dreams. I will never be alone again, alive or dead. I have five children. Nearly six. It hardly matters, I saw that phrase in a book once, 'Extracts from the Inquisitor's File.' An evil book. I never liked it. All the songs of my youth, all the things begun and never finished. What is the meaning of it all now? At this juncture, unable to sleep for the night. No preparation for the agony to come. Don't comfort me, don't put an arm around me, a leg across me. Leave me in peace. I will have sufficient strength for myself. Let me pace it out for myself, a racer at four in the morning, helmet in hand, stalking the circuit, which the crows hate. Leave me alone and give me strength for the race which must come upon me all too soon with its unknown result, and which cannot be called off for wet weather. In this land and place where only rooks are still speaking.

And later on, at seven, so many things to be done. The younger children rise, and one by one, creep downstairs to the dry. My lovely children with eyes that have seen the skies and the fields and the waves of the sea. Tell us you love us dad. We live our lives through you, dad, and the farm, and you don't want us there, and we are suffering. You should see your father, but you shan't see him if you set fire to the other lady's underwear on the line, no. They won't let you near the place. You have to be civilised before they have confidence in you again.

Children dancing up and down in the school bus. Do that in unison and you'll break the thing apart. I see their faces, expectant, golden. And there is mine, the only really bright one, clutching his cap to his side. They say he has the quick mind of the devil, and nobody would know he was just a Cornish lad. Haven't they heard the devil was a farmer? And we all buy grain.

The morning newspaper which, in a better world, would fall through the letterbox. But I have to fetch it for myself, since we sealed off the letterbox for our own safety.

Sometimes I think I never want to see that newspaper again, and it is such a waste of money. Sometimes I feel ecological about the trees. Sometimes I get upset about the filth on my hands. The print on my clothes, the words grubbing around in my mind. Corruption.

'Lois, Lois, Lois, my darling.'

'What do you want now?'

Wants his light trousers pressed. Going out. He has a ladyfriend. One with whom he talks about the world of Flen, and she listens without being annoyed.

'I don't do trousers, Tage.'

'Oh come on. I can't go out like this. They are not dry.'

46

No you can't go out in wet trousers, can you, and you don't know it yet, but your shoes had the hose turned on them this afternoon. I don't like playing dirty, but this is war.

Lois stepping down the hill, the baby jogging around in its pool, well up under the ribs already. Gasping at the bottom of the hill. Better going up than down. They say at the clinic that I have put on a pound, but am seriously underweight. So far so good then. A pound's as good as any other pound. Rest easy. Birth is not long. In my uncle's house, there was a picture of a cottage with cob walls, the roof no longer thatched, but of red galvanised iron. What was the sense of that? A house with no thatch, just a red iron roof.

By the cashpoint, a woman in a woollen hat, a lady from the hills, with no stockings, this clear, cold summer morning.

'Tell your fortune, lady?'

Lois, pressing buttons, choosing five pounds only.

'Sorry, no. Not necessary. I know my fortune. It's written on the front.'

'Eh?'

'Yes, I'm going to have a boy. That will be a blessing.'

'Lady, don't be sure.'

'Oh? You people normally know.'

'You'll never want, lady, and you will travel.'

'Yes, I know what you mean.'

'Your best friend has *m* and *r* in the name.'

'You're right, my friend.'

'Let me kiss you, lady, one day you will be famous.'

I know that, famous at the clinic, famous at the Doctor's, famous with Tage, famous with Davey.

My life is a ruin. My children fall from me and take my life with them. I am nothing. I am submerged under the clay-dust of my country. Who argues with the potter? I am fired by the sun, a mass of electrons, held together by somebody's idea. But not an idea of mine. And the final insult, I am unique.

This is another boy under the ribs, and I will spend another six months wondering.

There are her children, across the road there. Raw-faced, scarred, proud of their mother. The daughter does not have the gift, but a grand-daughter will have it. There will be no need to tell tales, bet on the *m* and the *r*, talk about travel, those old banalities. She will see things she would rather not see. And no, not even exploitation and the occasional beating will dull her wit. She will be fed right, and she will be healthy and able in her work.

I know that young lad over there will die unhappy and violently, and will burn in a fire. But I am no seer and I am unable to tell where or how. And to tell the gypsy at this juncture would seem an insult and a con. But I do know that for sure, as my name is Lois. And you, gypsy, are not entirely a fake, nor an ungifted one, which is perhaps why you step back now, and let me pass. I too hold the union card. Let me go. Do not spit upon me, though you have the right. I have not paid your toll. But I can't let you tell me your awful guff, not this morning.

'I haven't gone to school, mum.'

Oh well, the holidays are nearly upon us, and he was right to give himself up when he was caught, though I must confess I hadn't spotted the boy.

'I'm going home now, mum.'

'No . . . go back to school.'

'I'll go back after dinner. I'll be alright. Baxter hates me. Go on, mum.'

Eyes pleading. School should hold no terror these days. Not for good little boys.

'Come to the shops with me?'

'I'm supposed to be sick.'

'Go to the chemist, then, Peter.'

'For medicine, yeah?'

Conspiracy.

'You'll have to drink it.'

'What?' Grimace.

'You can't stay home from school, son. You have to go. Come what may, you can't escape it. And it only gets worse if you stay away. This is a civilised country. Everybody has to go to school.'

'Not if they're harvesting. I hate the subjects and the teachers. I don't learn nothing.'

'School was never for learning, boy.'

Edging away from me. Hating me too, my disloyalty. The hatred of the ages, the first love of the world. A schoolboy without a cap. Not one of my brightest boys. In a minute, he will escape me again. Nowhere to go.

'Goodbye, Peter.'

Running now, through the streets, dodging in doorways. All children do that, boy. I did it myself, and I'd do it now if it did any good.

But it wouldn't.

I am a matron, my children running all over the town.

'God is love.'

'Oh yes, but of course.'

I take a leaflet and nod, holding it in my hand, which sweats the print out of the paper.

'God certainly is love.' And the man beams at me, but he knows no more, poor soul, so I move on through the people who have come fairly early to town, for good vegetables.

'I think the prams in the pram shop are all very nice, aren't they, girls?'

'Oh, hello, Lois. Expecting again? Surprise, surprise. Thought you'd been done last time, like us. We're just looking. It'll be our daughter next, won't it?'

'Not by one of mine, I hope.'

'Oh, yeah, you 'ebm got no girls.' And she gives the envious eye, almost crying out. Watch her squirm. What a joy. At school, she was the first to go down. Now she wishes the same on her daughters. That first time she was pregnant, crying in the yard, the tar melting in the summer holiday sun. We had summers in those days. And didn't I feel good and righteous and fine?

'Now now, Hilda. That sun shines on all of us, good an' bad, quick and slow, great and small. We are all human. Are we not? I don't have the bother of girls, thank God. All that trouble.'

'Well . . . yes . . .'

Long time no see, friends. What made our valley so green? Not Tage's paint, no. The abundance of leaves in Autumn, weighing down the branches in summer, feeding the earth in winter. All gone now, under the housing estates. But, ah, my friends, my beauties, those leaves will cover the same walls and post-holes, and that office block, which makes a fool of our shrunken Roman walls, will tumble into the clay and lie forgotten as we.

A bus going by, top-heavy, green and swaying. Not so many of them around these days, and the numbers on them always being altered and rearranged. Ours is an alien country, with familiar people in it. And maybe I should let Tage the all wise in to my family, but he would wreck it and leave it helpless. Besides, he is not wanted among us. We are what we are because of the way we behave towards each other. It is something of a question of race, if I could only understand it. Not a question of finding the right contraceptive. Outsiders don't comprehend it.

In the bedroom it's an alien environment, an open field untilled. A little polite conversation. Are you reading this evening? Oh good. I'll finish the crossword if I can. An utterly private and utterly soiled world, facing his back, knowing nothing of this stranger in a land which will never become the paradise promised and vowed upon. I never wanted him and I never will. I wanted to be with my boys and their father and I do not understand and will never understand why I will never be able to bring them together again. Something in the psychology, or perhaps fate is working all the time here, as it is supposed to do.

And Tage pulling off an English cricket jersey, never having got the hang of the game at all. He told me there was nothing left between us. For my part there never has been anything between us.

'Our marriage will survive, you know, I see nothing to put an end to it. Do you know that people need reasons to let go in civilised countries?'

'You lack any sense of responsibility and decency, dear friend. I do not want my children brought up in this dirty, uncivilised country. Give me my blue tie with the narrow stripe.'

Passing the tie, smiling through the rain. Acid rain is the problem now, brought over from England to civilised, lazy countries. Tage upset by the language problem, not having nerves of piano wire, which is what is required around Lois, they say, though I can't say I have ever thought so myself. Tage calls it 'making love', perhaps because I am the wife. I never felt any bonus for that. The same old pumping trick with a sense of moral collapse. I usually have a priest in mind at the time. Passes the time pleasantly, as it has to be passed. At such times I should very much like to remember the special treat of it as it was in the very beginning of my maturity, the sweet-smelling grass, the orchard smells, but I suppose that sort of thing is available only to the memories of virtuous women. Bury me at the bottom of the garden where I have been happy and once tried to grow a magnolia or two, even in this climate. It seems that I will never get away. But I will. If only in the mind. And the mind is what counts. The quality of life is the quality of the mind. Take your opportunities where you can. Like that dreadful Robin Wakefield with no O Levels, out of work for four years, met a man on a station with two suitcases, one of jeans, another of paperwork. Said sell these, any problems ring me on 01. Rang him and no, he had gone. Went through the paperwork. A letter from Taiwan. Rang up Taiwan. Next thing he was buying the factory, buying fish and chip shops and petrol stations for something to invest in over here. And I went on teaching English to foreigners. Like Tage.

'Do you sometimes think of what will happen to us in the end?'

'Will there be an end?'

'Do you have, like Frank Kermode, a sense of an ending?'

'Let's not talk like that now. It is demoralising and leads to nothing, nothing at all.'

'Not at all. These things should be thought about.'

'No, they should not. Start thinking about things and then you start wanting them, whether you want them or not. Perverse, that is. No good can come of that.'

'So we wait then until we are beyond the grave, and we travel into the wilderness together because that is all there is to it.'

'I see no point in fighting any more. This is a kind of fighting. There is no need for it. It is like having a man behind you with a stick, beating your legs all the time.'

'Is it?'

'Why, yes of course.'

'Oh for God's sake, who gives a damn. Look at me now. I am worrying again.'

'I don't want to look at you.'

'Here I am. Do what you like.'

'If only you could be serious sometimes.'

'I am serious about everything. I wonder how you feel about the prospect of being with me for life. Myself, I don't like the idea, if it is to extend beyond the grave.'

'What nonsense. Incredible nonsense. Nothing is forever. I know it, somehow, and I think you know it too. Nothing between us is forever, though it is so amongst most of our friends.'

'I can't adapt to your friends or your way of life. You are dreaming if you think so.'

'I think so. I hope so.'

'What?'

'You were telling me a few evenings ago, how you get along with my mother and how you were sorting out a chest with her the other day, and you were very happy together.'

Lois clutching at her night-dress, watchful.

'No, no, I am serious. I heard you laughing together too. I heard you. I heard you both.'

'What are you telling me? Now you really are mad. As though I would sort out a chest with your mother. What sort of chest would she let me into?'

Tage laughed at the ceiling.

'Shut up, you fool. Always pulling my leg, and I am fool enough to listen to you.'

Lois watched him from the bed as he combed his hair with his fingers, short, strong, farmer's fingers. Too bad he was the wrong person, the wrong nationality, the wrong person altogether, since he had a certain attraction at this time of the day, pulling his shirt out over his trousers and tucking it in again, the pubic hair catching in the zip, bending slightly, leaning over the bed. I've heard you say, Tage, the best women know how to dress you, but I could never do that very well. You look alright the way you are.

Lois making an effort, rolling off the bed, standing in front of him, conscious of her worn out stomach, the foot with the broken veins. Bending forward to suck something.

'I am not used to that sort of thing from you.'

Holding his head in her hands, kissing the left shoulder which tastes of salt and soft soap. Biting the shoulder so as not to let the world see. The blue and white night-dress off, sitting on him on the edge of the bed. Now Tage, in Flen there is a farmer's table which is the right size to stand me against, or to stand you against, or to stand me across, I really don't mind.

'Oh my dear Tage. I have so many wishes.'

'And none of them for me.'

'I thought you were a fine man once.'

'I was never a fine man. I was a spoiled man who did what his mother asked because I did not know any other, and the all-weather combine harvester was always there with tinted glass and a stereo set. It all seemed quite natural, like driving a Lotus.'

'You ought not to stay with us.'

'That is my duty.'

'Which everybody expects?'

'Beyond all else.'

Lois taking hold of a long strip of wallpaper on the wet wall and tearing it off. At this juncture. And Tage such a tidy man. Kneeling across the bed with Tage upon her. The steam always gets to the coldest wall and makes it damp. Nothing to be done. Paint next time, in the new pastel shades. Making for a colder feel to the room. Other men do not have the same sense of proprietorship. This is a life which no-one reckoned on, not in the darkest moments.

'If we could be as we were in the early days.'

'Yes.'

'In the early days I could never wait for you to get home.'

'Quite.'

'Your grasp of English is superb now. But look, there is so much I want to ask you.'

Tage in his own inner world, enjoying himself regally. All the world slipping by, just staring into space. No-one can change the season, the avalanches in their time, the mist in its time and country. There were so many who did not know their country or what it all meant, and who lived and died in the perpetual bewilderment of the new-born. And this country is special, the one to which we return because we have to, loathsome as it is. The old landowner who could not resist the local council who took his mining land and made a garbage dump of it, thinking it to be derelict land, as though something in the north or the midlands. And there will be time, time for you and time for me, and time for a hundred planning decisions amendments and revisions before the taking of land and tea. He wore a white shirt and corduroys with the crotch hanging low in gentlemen's style and as he stood he cried out to the hillside as plain as day, 'This is the land which ye shall divide by lot. And neither the division nor unity matters. This is the land. We have our inheritance.' He shook his stick, the old dog cowered beside him. And I saw it all from my patch in the heather, across the valley. Not even his own Lord assented in that moment, and he was beaten, accepting cash for the worn out patch of our country. We were so rich then. But there were to be further humiliations, wrought not by the ordinary people, not even by the visible trend in politics. But by the graspers of the times, the ignorant, the uninformed. By the alien. And now it was my duty to avoid the alien and his children.

My people were my own people and I would not spawn any stranger. But I lived in his house even so, and I was one of those who compromised and lost everything in the process. His hand on my title deeds, his breath in my ear, my heart at my feet. On Porthtowan sands, scraping the tar from my ankle. We did not know then how much would be sacrificed, how much ultimately lost. So much fun to be had at the seaside. But the yellow rock of the uplands, which in the sun smelled of metal, oh that was a thing to contend with, a thing never to be forgotten, though taken from us, from all of us, for the last and final time. And Tage had fine hair, yellow and golden in the sunlight, the pump working as never so well before.

CHAPTER 7

'Lois, I am going to the bank today.'

'Let the kids go with you.'

'No, I've got business.'

'They'll stay outside.'

'They won't.'

'Go on.'

'How am I ever going to do anything, Lois, if I have to take your children everywhere like a nanny?'

'Swedish au pair. Tage, I've got all the washing to do. About five machine loads of it. If you don't want the machine going during dinner I suggest you get everybody out of my way, including the one dragging my shoes around the floor. Tage.'

'O Lois.'

'Why don't you go to the furniture shop and get me some furniture? This dreadful outer office stuff. This is not the dentist's. And you put your boots up on the so-called coffee table, when my boys aren't allowed to.'

'Just let me go to the bank.'

'Go to the bank, then.'

'I must go to the bank. I can't take the children with me. They get lost in town. They go away from me.'

'Don't be silly.'

'You turn them away from me, don't you.'

'Against me. I don't.'

'Swine.'

'Not swine. I took you from the swine.'

'Oh yes, from the nasty teaching job that paid nothing and was really miserable and boring, from independence and freedom to look after the children as I wanted to look after them.'

'I saved you from going back to your stinking cousin Davey, who never let you out of the back yard.'

'Utter rubbish. I should never have confided in you. I should have stayed as I was.'

'You saw me as a way out of a nasty situation. Having to work and work at your boring job, teaching the natives to speak English, never getting back to your children in England. I thought you were a good woman, badly put upon. I should have known. I was warned.'

'I'll bet you were. I bet you were really warned off me. And only your vanity made you have me despite your better judgement and mine, if it comes to that.'

'Alright, Lois. Let me go to the bank. I've had enough. I need a holiday in my own country.'

'You need a spell in your own country? I need a spell in anybody's country but yours and mine. I need a long holiday, a very very long long holiday, if you don't mind.'

'Alright, Lois, can we just be nice to each other for a last few days?'

'Oh yes of course, do let's be nice for a last few glorious days.'

'The children can come with me to the bank.'

'And will you go to the supermarket and get some meat for the freezer? It looks to me like a long winter coming. Take a big bag and get a taxi back. Get another computer for the boys and a lot of video tapes for me. And then I will be prepared to sit out another glorious few months of my youth.'

'I have to go to Sweden.'

'Be sure to telephone every day. So many things happen to people who are left alone, don't you find?'

'For God's sake Lois, I will come back again. I won't leave you here forever. You can always go back to Sweden with me. Why am I here at all, but for your sake?'

Slamming out of the door with no coat on, the womb tightening, making the head a little light. Not possible to stay there arguing about the bank with Tage. Walking up the road this time and around the crescent. Warm summer sun. This is the best time of the year, in the most beautiful place in the whole vast world. I will live and die here, my children too. I will never see that awful place again. I will never go back there with him again. I will suffer no more humiliations. See the little gardens, Penaluna's back bent towards the sun. As it should be.

Down the hill to the park. I shall be alone, alone again with a few quid in my pocket and peace in the bed. Able to kick out and find nobody there. In the autumn I will go to the Bournemouth Symphonietta concerts, booking very early, getting a good seat, leaving before the audience start cheering and stamping their muddy feet. This is the life. I will buy some French cookery books and learn to cook properly for the boys. No more nasty burgers but lots of French onion soup with those funny little toasty things floating on the top. New duffel coats for the winter. And won't he be so sorry not to hear from me? Yes. This time the little one will have a new cradle of its own with small flowers patterned in the linen. As the boys get older I will keep flowers on the glass table in a nice jar. People, nice people will call at the house. I will have a patio built like those people up the road and I will sit in the sun, my brood around me. I will ask Tage for money to send the boys to a real and proper school, where they will never learn bad tricks and get into trouble, but will spend their boys' energy on cricket, rock-climbing and mathematics. I will join an evening class and see whether I cannot learn something new and useful, like information and retrieval studies, computers and such like. I should like to join a creative writing class and learn to tell the world what I already know. I was smarter than the rest of them, with their mortgages and their link houses. Tage thinks I am thick, and I resent that. I stayed at home with the children because there were so many of them and Tage thought it was only right that I should. But I resent it so and I want to be free of it now. I will be free of it now. I was more intelligent than the rest of them at our school. None of them went to college like me. It's a great pity I was so silly to give up teaching. At least I kept my mind active. I don't know if I could study anything now. I feel so stupid, and Tage has a way of assuming I am stupid. He brings out the worst in me. It should have been Davey or nothing. It's like a death in the family now, with Davey gone. Or me gone from Davey. And no going back. Another lady there now, with wallpaper with blue roses, covering up the cracks from the subsidence. She won't last with him. But oh, she has done. She has lasted with him. That's the trouble. Shows no sign of moving. And he's a coward to keep her there. I would have turfed her out long ago. And she can't cook like me, nor wash, nor clean like me. And I was made for Davey, having something of the same blood in me. Summer sun. The long days and nights. The five-barred gate to the half-acre field, where we kept the horse when we could catch it. What a time that was, with the thatch falling in and the slates riffling off in the wind, clattering like elfin hoofs in the yard. It was a very good year.

Someone approaching. It was the doctor himself.

Been so worried about you, wondering where you were and what was happening to you, your husband and your children and your health. Shaking his head, looking sad and guilty. Taking off his tie and putting it in his pocket, settling down on the grass for a chat, rolling around in the grass for a chat.

'Hello Lois.'

Looking guilty, wondering whether to stop or to go on, leaving his trouble behind him forever. Never to think of it again.

'Oh hello.'

Looking casual, thick, dark circles under her eyes. Off colour.

'Haven't seen you for so long. Where have you been?'

'Not far.'

'Oh Lois, I waited for you in the cafe. I didn't know what had happened to you.'

A very nice young man, especially in a dark suit. I'll have my hands on you as soon as I can, if you will allow me the honour.

'I came, but you were probably on duty every time.'

'You could contact me at the hospital. They would page me.'

'Yes, but I wouldn't. Hospitals aren't for that.'

'True.'

'You can always telephone me.'

'I can?'

'Yes of course.'

'But you said your husband would . . .'

'Oh no, not any more.'

'Oh, that's good.'

Now go on with you. I've had enough. Go back to your duty. Where do we go wrong in bringing them up? Boys without fathers say they are deprived, and boys who had fathers tell of their fear and hatred of the old man, who was always home late.

Waving goodbye slightly. A little smile and he walks away, perhaps forever. Come back Doctor. I have a slight pain and an awful lot of itch. Oh do come back and play. This is really too bad, and the walk back up the hill is far too much without a reward.

Throw me a line. I have no anchor. My children are my anchor. Hold up the baby to its father. This is what I have made for you, in my suffering. I can't have him. He's not mine. This child is Tage's, isn't it. The doctor will dump me when he knows. He must know. They always know, these medics. But I want the doctor, not Tage. I must know where he lives and what he is really planning for his future. I can't let him go, just like that. I'll discuss it with him. There must be a way I can get out of this. The boy is single, he's not in the same fix as me. I am years older than him. If I could just get myself sorted out. Divorce Tage, run away, anything at all. But for the children I would go. Anywhere alone. Just to be alone again. With my cream suit and my new handbag. Like Marjorie, only with style and dignity. Get myself together and go. I feel it is time to go, even in this condition, even like this. I've been hard on poor old Tage. It's not all his fault. He's only a foreigner. Just a farmer, really. I must do something about myself. Dress up a bit. Put on a bit of weight. But I can't. I don't have any heart for it.

There was a light in the kitchen. Tage was cooking for the little children, nice big plates of beans and toast. He was so nice to the children, not his children, after all. So, doubly nice. They got in his way, but he cared for them. He had none of his own. Not until now, that was. And it wouldn't be too long now. All over the town men were making beans and toast for somebody else's children, all one in a million men.

'Tage, have you seen my hairbrush or my lipsticks?'

'In the drawer, all put away.'

'Been to the bank?'

'No. Been in the park?'

'Yes, lovely.'

'You smell nice.'

'I tell you, Tage, I think it is time I made more of myself ~ you know ~ smartened up a bit.'

Tage sat down on the Swedish sofa, his job for the day well done. Not having gone to the bank after all, the children happy and well fed now. Lois fetched her lipsticks, the red and the pink. I could have been an actress ~ anything. I had every opportunity before all this. I could have travelled the world, and would have done. I had opportunities. I kept turning everybody down. There wasn't plenty of time, there was no time at all. Whiskey kept the pain away only an hour at a time. Buried in this countryside. Get away from here, they said, such a small world, this Cornwall, where nothing grows and nothing works anymore. No factories, no industry, just rocks and gorse-bushes. No place for anybody with a future, with talent such as yours. What a beautiful lady, oh no not skinny, not scrawny, but rather beautiful, as you see. You don't think enough of yourself, dear. An awful lot of nice Cornish girls have made it to the top. You don't try hard enough, my precious. You're a bit on the old side now, of course. Those wrinkles and wobbly teeth. But a nice old girl like you, who went to the races and ran with the yearlings, well, a nice girl like you should have no trouble finding a better berth than this. This is no way to live. You could have your cream suit and navy handbag, your hats, your coats, your furs, your rings, your decent woollen coats, your nice little jumpers. You could have farmland to stroll in, acres and acres of it, with a lovely large farmhouse with dozes of irregular, well-proportioned rooms, all in the midst of nowhere. You could have it, have it all if you could ignore Tage, come to a compromise with him. You don't have to live with him and his mother. She won't last forever. She would compromise. Mothers do. She will accept you now. She will have to. There is no need to be afraid of her. For women, their children are their power.

Lois with a beaming smile.

'Brush my hair, Tage.'

'You haven't long hair.'

'Oh go on, Tage.'

'Don't be silly, Lois.'

'Tage, do you like long hair?'

63

'Yes, of course.'

'If I grew mine?'

'Long?'

'Shoulder-length.'

'You have short hair.'

'But if I grew it long?'

'Yes, I suppose, but . . .'

'But? Why do I always have to have short hair, must have short hair because it is short now?'

'Have what you like, Lois, I don't mind.'

'No. You don't mind. You don't mind what I look like. You don't look at me.'

'I like it short.'

'Of course you do.'

'What am I supposed to say?'

'You don't mean it.'

'I do mean it. But why not have long hair also?'

'A wig?'

'A wig or your hair. What does it matter?'

'Yes. I could have both.'

'Then I choose which Lois I fancy.'

'Why not, then?'

'Why not?'

'Why not? You could choose your lady, as you do now, and you wouldn't have to bother to get out of the chair, would you?'

'Oh come on, Lois, not that again. Give me a kiss.'

'Go away.'

'Lois!'

'Brush my hair, please.'

'Shall we go out?'

'Where? Restaurant? Cinema? Bingo?'

'Stop it, Lois. I try to please you.'

'Oh yes?'

'I wish you would not be awkward, Lois.'

'I'm not awkward. I'm just fed up. Fed up with you and the children and Toldhu Estate and everything and everybody. It's not your fault. It's me. I don't want to live like this anymore.'

'Like this?'

'Like this. Like this. I hate it here.'

'Well, what's wrong? What's the matter, Lois?'

'I don't want to be here like this.'

'Well, where shall we go?'

'I don't want to go anywhere with you. I shouldn't have got married again. All my instincts told me not to. Don't worry, it's my fault, not yours. I shouldn't be having this baby. It's one too many.'

'Come back to Sweden. It will seem different there. We have money there and good hospitals.'

'You want me to have an abortion, don't you? I told you before what I think of that. How dare you, you Scandinavian swine. Don't touch me, leave me alone. Go back to Sweden where you belong. I'll be alright. Just leave me alone. For pity's sake. I'll recover. I'll do something. I just have to get out of Toldhu Estate. But not with you. You make things worse for me.'

'Lois.'

'I don't know what to do. I've ruined my life. I shouldn't have married you or anybody else. I can't bear it here. I'll have to go away. Nobody can help me. Leave me alone.'

'What? What can I do?'

'Go away.'

'Go away?'

'I don't know what you're offended about. You were off to the bank today to get your money out and go. What a turn-coat you are.'

'What is a turn-coat?'

'Oh shut up. Leave me alone. Go back to Sweden.'

'What is it, Lois? What is really wrong? What have I done? It is my fault, isn't it? I should not have said I would go back home but well, I thought it might be a break for you and for me. What can I do to help you?'

'Never mind. Leave me alone.'

'I don't want to leave you alone, and you don't want me to go. There you have been putting on some lipstick for me, and doing your nails.'

'Quite.'

'And what would old Tage do without your children? And we're going to have one of our own now. Won't that be just what we wished for?'

'You're so right, Tage. So right. Blimey, what would I do without this pregnancy now? Stupid of me to think otherwise. Dear me yes. Make me a cup of tea, dear. At least you're not sterile like some. So many bring it on themselves, I always say.'

Lois dragged herself upstairs to sit on the bed, the heart thumping, the hand shaking. Not possible to cry, just this tightness in the chest. Most women have crying as the trademark but farming takes all that away from one. Best thing to do really is change the clothes and go out again. To get away from the atmosphere. Stifling in here. Perhaps the doctor has some time off at this point. She dropped her clothes on the little rose coloured slipper chair beside the wardrobe and looked at the clock. A quarter past six. Perhaps her friend the doctor would give her a nice cup of tea and have a brief, light chat with her. She would enjoy a nice light, polite chat now.

Feeling very guilty, face quite white. Sorry Tage I just have to get out of the house for a moment. You haven't done anything wrong. I am just so very full of misery, on my own account.

'You can't go out, Lois.'

Tage confused and frightened.

'I don't think you should go out again, Lois.'

'Sorry, Tage, I just have to get out of the house for a moment.'

What to do? Tage worried now, hoping for her company this evening. Lois fighting for breath, the door, a little freedom.

She walked slowly to the taxi. Much more fun in town. The dance-halls, the public houses. The latest tunes. Tage a terrible drag on one, wanting his children brought up on his farm, with its wood sheds and exemplary machinery. With Dobbin the damned horse and farm accountants in the family. He just wants an English wife, playing cards in the evening, going to concerts, driving to town in the Volvo along the dirt roads with their pot-holes the size of shafts. It's all very well, but the Swedes are very different from us, not the same sort of people at all. For one thing they are so peculiar. I don't want my children brought up there, not with those people. For one thing, I like to be able to belt the boys when they do something wrong. I don't want to be prosecuted for disciplining them. Moreover, moreover, I don't want to be snowed in half the year and have to sit by the lake with the mosquitoes for the other half. I want to eat butter, not margarine on my bread. I want to drink Cornish milk and eat Cornish pasties. I want my boys to know who they are.

That's enough ranting. Outside the hospital, looking for the doctor. That terrible place, the maternity unit. Groans coming down the corridors to greet you. Makes you shudder to look up at the windows of those side rooms with their dim lights. Seems like the end of your life towards the end, when there is some question of whether you will get through it alright. Those nursing sisters may as well wring their hands and watch television, for all the good they do. After all their interfering, nothing is known about birth, what brings it on, what reverses the processes. Plenty of insight is offered in those moments: 'Why the hell did I do it when I was happy as I was?' And then the silence from the front, another soul formerly competing with the workings of your brain, now out into the world, crying with its own lungs. And you all alone forever. Until the next time. Sink into the rubber mattress in the iron bedstead and wait for that moment when somebody says that wonderful word, 'discharged', and home you go.

Into the front entrance of the main building. Lots of people here. The WVS counter with teddy bears, chocolates and story books for the dying and their children. Must get to see the doctor. What is his name again? Doctor Stephens. Doctor David John Stephens of ear, nose and throat. Yes of course he is off duty. No I am not a private patient. Are they joking? In my condition. What do I want with nose, ears and throat? He has invited me to dinner, as usual on a Saturday night. I am not a nurse, you know. These receptionists all the same, trying to answer the telephone and define your morals at the same time. I am a little early, thought I would go and meet him at his flat. No I don't know where his flat is. That is why I find myself at Reception bothering the likes of you. I see, left at the cross-roads beside the barrier and the empty sentry box. Thankyou so much. You could have saved a lot of fuss by telling me in the first place.

At the cross-roads, by the sentry box. Into the block of flats. Up to the third floor. First on the right.

Ring the doorbell. No panic. No problem. Go away again if he is with a nurse. Just called to say hello, just as you asked me to, when I was passing. Answering with a cheery call. Obviously expecting somebody. Oh dear, not pleased, I can see it on his face. Doesn't know how to disguise it, either. Never mind. Quite a gentleman really, and good looking.

'Good God.'

'Hello.'

'What are you doing here?'

'Just passing. You reminded me to come and see you.'

'Warming, but obviously expected a nurse any minute now.

'Please, come in. I was going out for a drink.'

'Well . . .'

'Please, come in.'

'Well, I was just passing. This is clearly not the time.'

'Where were you going?'

'Just came out to see you.'

'Especially?'

'Yes. But of course it doesn't matter. I wasn't invited. It's Saturday evening.'

'No no. You misunderstand. I was only going with some friends in the hospital. Nothing that can't be postponed.'

'Oh well . . .'

He sat on an institutional armchair, with its thin, cup-scarred wooden arms. She sat on the matching sofa.

'Why don't I take you out for a drink? You can drink orange juice.'

'Why not?'

They went downstairs in the lift. She stood in one corner, he in the other. Taking her hand for an instant, letting it go on the ground floor. Into the underground carpark, where his very first green sportscar stood, with its dials, its leather gloves and its compass. Voices of nurses and young doctors, porters and kitchen staff off duty, lounging against walls, getting into cars, driving away from the institutional smells of the hospital.

'I am having a baby.'

'I can tell.'

'I have enough trouble.'

'You do?'

'I just don't want to go anywhere obvious, where people can see me out with you. This is very tricky.'

'Terrific.'

'I'm sorry, David.'

'Please don't rub it in.'

'It's a fact.'

'What?'

'My baby.'

'Oh yes.'

What a problem. Shouldn't have done this. There will be a whole pile of trouble with Tage now. He always suspected. Somebody will tell him now. He will deny paternity. Let me out of this silly Lotus. I should go home before I get into trouble. I don't know this young man, anyway. He isn't too pleased with me as it is.

'Do you like this hospital?'

'I hate it.'

'Why?'

'Oh, it's rather backward for a teaching hospital.'

'And where do you want to settle?'

'Oh, I don't know. Somewhere like Cornwall, but with a better hospital than this one. There are much better hospitals than this one. I just got stuck down here, for the moment. It's alright for the moment, though. Especially with you down here in Cornwall. I never thought for a moment you would come to see me.'

'Like this.'

'Yes, like this, as you say.'

'Are you pleased?'

'Very.'

'How long will you stay in Cornwall, then?'

'A few more months.'

'And then?'

'I will have to earn some money.'

'Oh well, I will have to make the most of your being here, while you are here.'

'What difference will my going make to you?'

'Well, I suppose the joy will go out of my life. Certainly the excitement will. I shall have to stay home with the children, and I will have another to look after.'

'A bad time for you. It's a pity I can't take you with me, wherever it is I am going, that is.'

'Take me with you?'

'Just an idea. A nice thought. I like to think I could take you with me if I really wanted to. If you had no husband and children. If you were really as carefree as you seem, walking in the park, throwing stones into the pond. Having a coffee with you. But I suppose it's all an illusion. You are probably as beleaguered as the rest of us. I always imagine that you are really happy and carefree, though.'

'You do?'

'Of course I do. It's the only thing that keeps me going on a Wednesday afternoon, the idea that you are content.'

Sitting there in the Lotus. Just sitting in a most uncomfortable position, a great deal of strain on the back. The children go with me, of course. The sudden idea now, that he thinks about me as one of those in the category of needing his protection. One of his herd. One of those he could be troubled to cut out and keep as his own. I am not sure that I could manage it. Not sure that I would want it, with all my children. Couldn't he just move in with us when Tage was gone? No, life is never easy like that, and men always want to make things as difficult as possible, not admitting to their arrangements. There would never be enough money. He would hate the horrid children. I would have to have four more. My health won't stand that now. What are you like off-duty, doctor? Are you spoiled? Do you put your feet on the table and drink lagers from tin cans?

They had a drink in the local public house, just down the road, where all the other medical persons drank their drinks. It was a good sign, Lois felt, that he did not drive to somewhere in the country, with velvet seats, to hide her away.

Off again, into the country now. Into Carncos and the Redundant Miner. Settling into burgundy and pink seats, seats for whores and businessmen who would never come here. Surrounded by clerks on their wedding anniversaries.

People in Marks and Spencer suits looking at them and nobody remarking. A waitress in black showing them a foolscap menu decorated with sketches of picks and shovels. I'm not hungry, David.

Oh surely, madam, a little scampi in golden breadcrumbs?

So, reading the menu with David John, being steered away from irradiated seafood for the sake of her health. Why could we not have gone to The Experimental Oyster? But we came here.

The chair she sat in, like a burnished throne. Sickness came with ease now, just a speck or two on her dress, the lavatory door open to the washroom and the sounds of water running from taps into shell-pink basins. My hair needs washing, really, now that I've been sick. The smell of it gets everywhere. The end of a perfect evening. Even before I could finish the flan. Perhaps they will wrap it up for me and let me take my piece away. It was good of you to take me out. I needed a change. Sorry I got sick. Just one of those things that happen now and then. Just one of those things. Again? We will have to work out something official. I can't go on doing this.

He took her home. She said goodbye at the end of the Crescent. He left the car and walked down behind her in the shade. After a while, a light went on briefly on the upstairs landing. Its warmth spread across the wastes of the sky, knitting up the darkness: and then it was all night. Thinking about it, the young man began to cry unexpectedly.

CHAPTER 8

Summer. It will all be over soon, they tell you. Life burgeoning everywhere. But autumn overlays the summer. The roses blown and fallen. I lie in bed in the morning. The children are out of school. I hear them in the road outside, swinging cricket bats and kicking hell out of each other. I do wish they would be quiet. Shut up and go away. I hate them coming in wet and muddy, the leather of the boots cracking and falling away from the uppers. The crust on its Swedish uppers. That is what they have brought Tage to. Why don't the children just go away? Do I have to listen to them here from my bed for the rest of my days? Is it much of an advantage to be an invalid? Is it better to be well?

Tage doesn't like it very much, this sickness. Not used to it. Generations of sturdy, blonde, cheerful people around him, with not too much brain. Plenty of ham from the smorgasbord and a ride on the ferry twice a year to Denmark. Bringing home cheery pictures of people beside windmills in clogs. Not this sickness.

Getting out of the bed carefully. There should be no sickness now. Not at this stage. Should be bursting with vitality, full of lettuce and tomatoes. Creeping into the bathroom, head steady, careful not to look down. Like standing in the bow of a car ferry in a storm. The trick is not to look down. Downstairs next and put on the electric kettle for a cup of coffee. Tea makes me ill now. That best, most homely, yet exotic drink in the whole world, now makes me ill.

Let me out of this, Lord, in the most pleasant way possible.

And sitting on the pert metal kitchen chair, springing slightly as she leans forward, Lois thinks over the void of the month before, when doctor David John took her out in the Lotus ever so briefly, and the sickness started. What dignity now? And he didn't say goodbye or how wonderful, or hope to make arrangements to see you again. Just roared away in the night, leaving me sick as the cat. Never to return no more no more. Never to return no more. Is there anybody out there with the same experience?

Into the waiting-room lounge. Marjorie's sofa looks ridiculous now in this glassy room. I liked it so much. Poor old Marjorie. I wonder how she is. Not a sign nor a sound. Nothing from Penaluna either. Thought he would have been around here, blaming me, the bad influence on his wife. But no, nothing. Nothing from the doctor, nothing from Marjorie. Thank God for one's husband. So much for friends. A person like me needs friends. So much for Marjorie. So much for Doctor David John. Tage is out all the time these days, with nothing to do. Ought to start a little business and take up golf if he wants to stay here. All this lounging about is no good for him. He will get into a terrible state.

So, Lois is going to have another baby. Six in all, that will be. Where are my proud parents, my brothers and sisters in their Sunday clothes, coming on a visit? Nowhere. Where is my old Davey? Nowhere. Looking at the photographs in a dusty album kept in a drawer. There is Marjorie at work in the garden, leaning on a rake, with Penaluna bending over in the background. There is Marjorie bending over in the garden with a shears in her hand, Penaluna in the background standing up, staring into the camera. All fairly scintillating. There are Marjorie and Penaluna at a Dinner and Dance. Tee hee. Marjorie, in some sort of frock and the white pointed shoes she had for her wedding. There are Marjorie and me on Billy Nankivell's old donkey at Porthtowan. Ha ha. And there is Billy again with the donkey and a pile of children. What days they were! We never go to the beach now, except in wellingtons. Too much dog poo. First it was the tar and oil. Now it's sewage and animal shit. When we were kids, nobody could go to the beach on a Sunday in case the chapel people found out and your parents got an earful. It's all changed now.

A morning of lightness and brightness, with the snapshot album, avoiding the wedding album and other realities. At this time of the day, children going home for their mid-day pizza and crispy fry pancake. There could be nothing more charming than this corner of the world, this light, bright, convenient little house on the corner, with the little copper beech now past its best and the big, bright autumn flowers already on their way out.

Into the kitchen again, to stir up the bubble and squeak for the children, the remains of last night's roast dinner. Everybody sitting around, my dark-eyed ones. Ignoring the fact of Tage being out in the town somewhere. Ah well, we all know what he is like. There is always tension when he is there. The children's chatter is so much sweeter when he is gone. The muscles in my legs giving me trouble now. Cramps which make life a misery. Especially during the long, long night, when the worry sets in and the dawn is a desert away.

Clearing up the plates and drinking coffee splashed with milk from the refrigerator. I could be alone like this always, Marjorie gone and Tage out of our lives for good. The pain would soon go.

They had met just a few times ~ regularly, in the Green Apple coffee house, and then casually, in the park or by the river. Always by accident. She had no way of knowing whether there was any significance in it at all. It was better if there was no significance in it. He seemed naive, young, a potential bore, blinkered and uninteresting. He also represented a way out of a predicament. A reason for and a means of saying goodbye to Tage, in the nicest possible way. And for some reason, he seemed crazy about her, though he must have known she had little intelligence and less breeding: a potential life-long embarrassment with an awful number of hostile children. A way out of this tiny house, with its cheap pots and pans and its electric stove with the four rings, its calendar on the wall.

No longer a question of falling in love, not after all these years, when the cracks begin to show, and man's face is no longer his fortune. Nothing about it is sound now. Nothing one can trust. They come and go, giving each other in marriage and being given in marriage, until the fatal day. The only thing to do is to till the garden.

Lois lying on the bed again, in the afternoon. It was all an unhappy experience, from the university to Toldhu Close. I was never happy with any of it. A few brief months of joy with the babies, ruined because of others who thought this and that about Davey. And the handover to Tage Af Klercker from Davey. All too sudden. A great shock to the system. My Cornish parents, struggling through the days, the lamp cracking in its own heat, in the long twilight. If I could live again, I would not live to see them part and I would not live to see a stepfather enter the home. But that very thing I did to my own children. Because nobody else was there to help us. Now, lonely and bored, with money in the bank, I lie here on his horrid double bed and weep about it all. I have not the right.

Don't worry about us now, dear Doctor. Here I am, in my silly little house, huddling with my children, waiting for the end. I have had some good things, some good times in the past, little joys and excitements. More excitements than joys, of course. You haven't telephoned this week, and I haven't telephoned you either. Too many folks in between, curious and professional. Neither of us want their remarks and their jokes. Not with me in this present condition. If I could get away from this house with my children. Without the paperwork.

Without the paperwork.

The cramps in the leg forced her out of bed again. She made another hot, milky drink. Opened a packet of biscuits and ate the lot.

At five o'clock it was time to think about making the dinner again for the children. I am being strangled by the mixer. Asphyxiated by the flour, overcome by the eggs. Let's not make toad in the hole after all. How did I ever ever get into this monumental mess? When I surface again, where will I be? How old will I be then? Was it just a dreadful miscalculation that got me here?

Doctor David John was so nice. He seemed to be trying to fit in some sort of promise, some sort of offer of a way out. Before he got out.

I was sorry about it, Tage. It was just one of those things. I rather liked the man. He was young and sound and was out to do the right thing, with a little wife of his own, trying to make the best of the universe as he found it. You couldn't blame him. The fault was in me. Wanting to reciprocate. When I was lying, it was only to go into the Green Apple, after all. It was not to set up some outrageous conspiracy.

Tage, what can I say? After all, it was not to set up some conspiracy against you personally.

They seemed like wonderful days now, soft and warm, those few days with the doctor. In memory, the rain seemed irradiated by a kind of starlight. The sunlight penetrated all the gloom and there were no perplexities. No trying to understand one another's game. It was all laid out like the pieces on the chessboard. And the pieces themselves were enough to rejoice in. The cruel game itself ceased ever to have been played. The town was bathed in glory. The Green Apple was a shrine to the most glorious and best the galaxy had to offer a man and a woman. And that was all Lois felt able to occupy her mind with.

She would have loved to have gone out. Just to take the bus and go into the hills for a day. To listen to the women from the hills as they came in to the market. She was so sick of reading her magazines, the ones which encourage women in their stupidity, buttress them in their self-importance and righteousness regarding copper bottomed pans and gas safety in the kitchen. At this stage, there should have been resignation, cheerfulness. The hormones should have been working on her by now, shielding her from all misery.

In bed at night, unable to rest, having been in bed most of the day, Tage attentive but thoughtful, still finding some relish in her body. Lois dry, weary, her tones plaintive, no longer quarrelsome or cocky.

'Poor old Tage.'

'Me?'

'Poor old Tage.'

Lois speaking in her sleep, pulling at the crinkled sheet, on the edge of tears.

'Is there anything wrong, Lois?'

There was nothing wrong, nothing wrong with the pregnancy. But there was something at the back of her mind.

'What is it, Lois?'

'Something is wrong with me. This is not going as it should. I know about these things. I am an experienced mother.'

'Well, of course you are, but . . .'

'I am sick . . . weary in some sort of way.'

'How?'

'You are here with me, but I feel so alone. As though I was deaf.'

'Well, you are certainly not deaf.'

'I know, but that is how it feels now . . . distanced from this house, and from life itself.'

Lois pulling at the sheet in the darkness. All alone inside herself.

'Perhaps, after this baby, you need to do a course . . . go back to college, some training . . . I will help with the baby. My baby.'

'No, Tage. You don't understand.'

'Please. I sometimes think you still do not love me.'

'I don't.'

'Lois, you destroy my feelings. I find it difficult to say anything to you when you are so . . . I didn't mean to be born Swedish. I try to make up for it. If I could be a Cornish farmer, I would be one. But it is not possible, is it? It is not my fault I am what I am. I won't upset you more than I can help but I find it so difficult with you.'

'I can't ask you to stay with me any longer, Tage.'

'But I want to stay.'

'I don't.'

'No, we must stay together now. Now that you are having my baby. You are my wife. I don't mind staying at home while you go out for a drink, with your friends. On a Saturday. I understand that. You always used to. All I ask is for us to keep our house together. I think it is best. I have thought about it as well as you.'

'We don't get along, Tage.'

'Yes we do. And we will. In Sweden. In this country. We will have a holiday and spend a few days in the sun. We have never done that. We have spent the summers apart because of the farm. But now we will spend all summers together. Without any difficulty. We will enjoy it. We will go to Greece every year, like everybody else. We are a family now. The children will enjoy it.'

'I don't think so.'

'Come on, Lois.'

'No.'

'Look, you are always putting me off. I am trying to look after you and keep the family together, our family, our new family. I like us to be together. I should not have gone away before this. I will be a changed man. Everything will be alright. I will not go away again. It breaks the family up. The children don't accept me that way. I find it hard to stay here, but I will not, from now on.'

'Will not what?'

'I am saying I will not find it hard to stay here. The children will be ours and it will all be different.'

He put his arms around her and pushed his head against her breast, leaning on her, creating more tension than before. A small cry of despair from somewhere deep inside her mind, unformed, blurred at the edges, an animal despair, her fingers tightening and beginning to freeze on the sheets.

She would wake at five and earlier, the dawn lighting the narrow-paned windows, throwing a square of light on the tightly drawn curtains. From all corners of the concrete block building she could hear the children breathing. I am so tired of trying to work things out, calculating every move with and without Tage. Cornwall, Sweden, Cornwall. The hills, the valleys, the uplands, the lowlands.

Every morning, Tage drinking coffee, eating bread rolls rendered with some sort of margarine, for the sake of his heart. Lois downstairs in her blue dressing-gown which Tage bought her for the hospital. This is awful. I don't want this. I hate Tage being here. Why doesn't David John telephone me? He doesn't give a damn. None of them do. Only Tage. And I want him out of the way. Right out of the way. I want him back on the ferry with the lorries. Send him right back to his mother. That's really the best. Tage will never thrive here, will never survive here. I don't want to be here myself, but at least the place is mine and belongs to me. It won't harm me. But it will certainly harm Tage and his like. Not the sort of place a man like Tage would ever survive in. Not very conducive to life, these arsenic fields of home. Here, you can smell the rock. It seeps through the aftershave, masking the American musk of Max Factor and the rest of them. The poisoned personalities of the villages. Ah but this is the life. This is the life. But only for us. Not for them, those strangers. Like Tage. He will never fit in. Never fit in. Nor that David John person, the Doctor. Better let him go and forget all about it. He won't do us any good either. Not Doctor David John, no. Time to go home, Tage. Time to go home, friend. Your old mother at the door, waiting for you to stagger back in, full of lager. Leave me to the lanes, the leafy lanes of home. Of dearly beloved summer, now gone, when there is not a brown or curled edge anywhere. Little blond children running around. The six o'clock news read in broad daylight. Oh give me a home where the foxes and all sorts of creepy crawlies roam. I am getting hysterical. Seems to be the high blood pressure. Yes, we have blood pressure. Everybody has it. Everybody still alive, that is. And out there are the islands. The islands with the white sand, the fortunate islands which pretend to be tropical sometimes in high summer. What a wonderful place. But reserved now for the nobs of yore and today's yobs of another shore. With their shiny yachts. Pleasure-tripping. Why was I not born on those islands? I would never have left them. And then I would have suffered. More than I now suffer. To be exiled in one's islands. Ah, that is quite a thing. So much worse than being here and having a deep-seated grudge against one's continental neighbour. Well, I say there is nothing to be done. They are planting all of our gardens with gaily painted gnomes, and no-one can prevent them.

Lois suffered for several days, before Tage tried to call the doctor. She went out a few times for a can of beans, a pound of onions, but most of the time she sat at home staring into space. Tage brought her a woman's magazine, but that seemed to exacerbate her mood. She seemed to be turning into a very different sort of person for a while. Until, in the afternoon post there came a letter from her dear old friend.

Dear Lois

>*I thought I would just write and tell you how I am gettin on here in the capital city of London. Well, I got a job right away in a take-away but I didn't take home enough so I had to get another job and then another one on top of that. Then I was earning nearly about enough. I was staying with this man I met on the train but it got a bit too much what with him being so untidy and all, so I moved out to a place called Highgate. It was just a room in somebody's big house really, but that was alright. I was getting back too late at night, and getting up too early in the morning, what with my three jobs, so I thought I would look for a place closer to work, but that has been a bit difficult I can tell you. I aren't sure what I am up here for but I know it will come along soon, tha's what everybody say anyhow. I can't believe how friendly the people are up here and generous, not like down in Cornwall. I met the Shake of Araby last night at the bus stop. He just got out of a big black car, bigger than a taxi and went in the station. I couldn't believe it, he come right up to me. Anyhow he asked the way and I told him I didn't know as I was a stranger from Cornwall which I was surprised he didn't know where Cornwall was. His name is Omar Sheriff and I am going to have dinner with him tonight just for the fun of it. I shall be alright because his sister will be coming. In a place called the*

Connawt which sounds a bit Irish to me. Anyhow he said the food would be good even if it is Irish, which will suit me as I have been eating the take away stuff because I haven't got no time to cook. I was wondering how my old man is getting on, and will you go up and see him for a minute or two if you have got the time, Lois, I know you are about to have another baby or two. Good luck with that old dear. Well all these men about is driving me crazy but now I have got a Shake of me own I shall be alright thank God. I don't know how Penaluna would have took to me going away and all. I should like you to find out for me and I will look out for your letter in the post office. I am moving about so much I would rather not give you my present address. You will understand. I realise it's make or break for me now and I want to do the best for meself before it is all too late. Me white shoes is holding up quite well. I am still looking out for the ultimate which Stanley Penaluna wasn't able to give me, poor soul, so let's hope all goes well for me. To tell the truth, I am a bit sick of London, what with all the moving around but the time will come when I will be able to have my own little house up here like they little houses in Chelsea. No problem with them up there. I met a girl who was a maid in one of them. What a lark. In this part of the century too. The things you see up here. Incredible luxury and awful bad things on the streets. Still, the thing is to keep going. I bet you thought I would never find a job or a place to stay. Well the only trouble is finding a proper place to stay. Makes it all less worthwhile when you don't have nowhere permanent.

I am alright but the trouble is money. I could live down in Temarle and sail down to get my fish and chips in Gweek if I had the money in Cornwall I am earning here. But the trouble is the housing do take all the money. Without a husband and family I can't get no council flat neither. Anyhow dear, I will say goodbye for now as I am in the middle of getting ready to met Omar the man from Oman as he calls himself. Quite a lark don't you think. We are going gambling afterwards.

Well dear, I will close now. Will you have a peep at Penaluna now and then for me and let me know what's going on down there. Cornwall do seem so small now. But I shan't forget you at Christmas.

(Mrs) M Penaluna

The lined paper drifted across the bed during the day. Lois referred to it often, sometimes chuckling, sometimes frowning. Marjorie would add to the weight of her mind, whether she wrote to Lois or not. It was inevitable. Until Marjorie drifted home or . . .

Will I ever get better? Will I be handicapped for the rest of my years ~ Tage always fetching the shopping? Marjorie will have her problems but she will come through. See a bit of life. Having a good time. Loving every minute. She doesn't know how good she has it now. You never know until it is over.

This is a wonderful month, and a wonderful year. My year of contentment. The summer sun beating down bravely upon the bijou estate of Toldhu. Could anybody want better?

Tage called the doctor, who came and could find nothing wrong, and who looked as though he thought Tage nothing but a hysterical continental who had never seen a nasty, uncooperative woman before who was making the most of her transient condition. Lois refused to be taken into the hospital, so it was all a bit of a waste of time, and the doctor said that he would come back only when she was willing to co-operate. She could die of toxaemia, ha ha, but Lois was an old hand at this game and knew the fool was either incompetent or joking. The problem now was Marjorie, how to rescue her from this bed of pain and cramp with no telephone and no means of finding her. And I am really far too old to be a lady mother now, and perhaps I will die or there will be something wrong with it. I refused that test. Thousands of them go wrong. Cripples all over the place. Especially from mothers of my age. The misery of life. Tage wants to eat me and I am in this condition. When you get as old as I am, having a baby, well it can be serious. Geriatric motherhood.

And in this room, the wallpaper peeling and the plaster cracking. What can I do to make things better? Have the newspapers delivered every day. Give myself a treat. I have eaten every piece of fruit and every salad possible. I have peeled all the plums and put all the sweet papers on the side of the plate. And now it is time, I think to go into the dark. Or, I must just see Doctor David John tomorrow. Just one more time.

CHAPTER 9

Daybreak. One of the loveliest sights from this window. The eastern sky poised, warming up, like a valve in an old radio receiver. Just ready to sing. I sat upon the shore fishing, with the arid plain behind me. Shall I at least set my lands in order? Get thy house in order, for thou shalt die and not live. Damyata. The birds moving swiftly, directly, with such purpose. At the dawn of day. If this was one of my last days on this earth and I knew it, I would want to see an intriguing friend. But not if it was likely to cause pain, because I would want to remember that friend as he was, to the last moment of all. So now, is that why we do not act as though this were our last day? Of course, of course it would be unbearable if we had no expectation of tomorrow. Please, no more palpitations of the heart. If he was at all interested in me he would come here. He has not been banned from the house by an unbalanced Tage. Nor by me. He is just not concerned with us, has no part in us. If he came to the door, he would not know what to say. He has no history with us. I know how it is with him. And he has a professional attitude, a trained mind. He would not come. Not if I were dying. Somebody else would come then, of course. I would like his hand on my arm again, the light, polite touch of him. I will never know why. I have no means of knowing why. Drinking the wine of my fornication, but no not with this one. Playing it carefully, slowly, playing for permanence. And failing. Because I played it that way, and not some other.

After the birds, the city begins to stir, to stir in the corruption of all its yesterdays. Blinds going up, curtains drawn back. One more day. There is no going back. No yesterday before us. Only today. If we are fortunate. And if you were to ask me now, in my cage, taunted by the ever-present, overwhelming question posed by a boy, I would say, with her of Cumae, 'I only want to die.' The voices of the morning fade into these homely ones of children. I am a mother, and wanted here.

I will wait a moment longer. I will put off the time when I must face my emptiness in his unbelieving eyes. I will not leave my illusions and go down into the town to my humiliation, to my knowledge of failure.

'So. You have come downstairs. You are better now. I see it in your face.'

'I look brighter?'

'Much brighter.'

'Are you frying bacon?'

'Yes, oh yes, bacon and eggs. Smoked bacon for us, ordinary for the children. Will that be alright? You can eat fried things again? Remarkable. Very good.'

'I think your breakfasts, Tage, are the best in the world. Nobody fries an egg like you. A very delicate operation. Top chefs are given the job of frying an egg as an interview for a job at the Connaught. Oh yes.'

'I thought I would give everybody a fry. Good for them. Growing boys.'

'I don't feel right, you know. Still don't feel right.'

'What is it, Lois?'

'The pain is in the heart. Not being able to come to terms with it. With us having another baby. There is something wrong inside me. I don't want to bother you and the whole street with it. I wish it would go away, but the feeling never stops, from dawn to the end of the day and the middle of the night. I never know when I will be asleep now. Never know when I can sleep. I spend too much time in bed and I can't sleep at the right time.'

'What has upset you?'

'Not money, not us. Just life. I feel I can't take life. There is nothing wrong with us, no more than with other people. But

I can't take life as it is, here or in Flen. I can't understand it. If I could, I wouldn't be telling you about it like this.'

'Oh, your mother is dead, all your children are Davey's except mine, and now you have to think about having mine. It is difficult for you, Lois, but you will be alright. You will not commit suicide. Not this time. That is the life, as you say. Please do not think about it any more and old Tage will make the breakfast for everybody. Tage loves you all. Don't worry any more.'

'Back to Flen in the autumn, then?'

'What me? How can I do that now, unless you are able to travel. Fit and well.'

'Does that mean we have to stay here, then?'

'Lois, I don't know. I have to go back sometime. But there is the question of the boys' schools. Richard is not at an easy age. One day we will decide. There is more work in Sweden. Someone must run the farm one day. I do not have a brother. These things are important to my family. I have a family too.'

'Yes, that is true. I do so admire you.'

'Very good.'

'OK, sweetheart.'

'Eat up.'

Tage making breakfast for Davey's children. Jugs of orange juice. Toast under the grill. And not one of them at the table, their boots on the glass coffee table, their tapes and records over the floor. Your threshing machine lies rusting in the dark corner of a red wooden shed in Europe, Tage. And what was it your unofficial grandmother told you a decade ago, over which you pondered and could not find the answers, Lois? Yes, yes, this was it: Davey will pass away from your life. Your blood is too close. But not before time. The children, I have to say this dear, or I will perish too, understand I do not want to say this, the children will have no issue, and you will both outlive each one of them. But another will come late in life. You will resist. But, as you are my blood, I am telling you a secret now. Do not stand like an oak or you will fall when the hurricane comes. Do not you build a wall for weeds of jealousy to grow in, or in time men will scale you easy. They will get inside your fortress of rock and burn you out. Then there will be nowhere to go for you. No. Learn the ways of the marsh. Stand in the marsh, my dear, and bend with the reeds. No-one will penetrate you, and you will endure. There will be the mist and the birds to keep you company. You will endure. Any other way, Lois, is death. But you will not save the children. God knows, I endure the knowledge of this in my lifetime, and you and Davey are both my grandchildren. Your children are all mine. Do you understand me? No, of course not.

Silly old fool.

Now, the food sticking in Lois' throat. This was it. The root of the trouble. Grandma Davey the seer. Her witchcraft. She wished them dead, all of them. They violated her principles, and she never saw them again. It was all too much for the poor, suffering old soul.

But the reeds . . .

'Very nice. Very nice, sweetheart. No, I can't eat any more. Heartburn.'

'Oh.'

'And now, I think I will change and go into town for a little shopping. Been up in the bedroom far too long.'

'I know you have.'

'Just to get a nursing bra.'

'Oh well I will stay with the boys then. No good trying to help you with these things.'

'I think that's very sensible of you, old Friend Tage.'

'I will be here waiting.'

Waiting like a woman. So now he is tamed. For what? Old fashioned farmer in a pair of jeans.

'Oh, dear Lois. I love you, you know. Very much indeed.'

'It's only this baby.'

'Is it?'

'It will look like you.'

'So, it will also look like my wife Lois.'

'That's me.'

'Do you have any regrets?'

'None at all.'

'Do you have everything to go into the hospital with? Need another dressing-gown? You have been wearing this one.'

'I wore it right away, that's all. I didn't save it up for the moths. I might have been dead before I could wear it.'

'You have strange, morbid ideas.'

'And you are a fool to stay in this house waiting for me. It's not natural. You should be home on the farm. At this time of the year, especially.'

'Well, I don't think about it that way.'

'That's the trouble, Tage, you don't. And then, when the crunch comes you will be wondering what happened.'

Tage poured tea from the old metal pot into a glass cup. The glass sparkles in the sunlight, but the heat is soon gone. And too many of them crack before long.

'Let us not worry about this any more. It is so depressing. I don't ever want to start thinking about our relations together any more. Just about where we are going out to dinner. When seven o'clock comes I want you to get into the car and just take me out. You decide where. I won't be sick.'

'You're a good woman, Lois.'

'There was only one good woman, Tage.'

'Really.'

'And the Protestants seem to dispute that.'

But Lois was not well enough to go to town alone, so Tage came with her, and she was glad, all of her ideas about seeking out the good doctor David John having left her with

91

her strength. She panted around the shops, up and down the stairs, a small smile on her face, her hand sometimes pushing back the hair from her eyes. Tage said he would pay for her hair to be cut, but she could not allow it, and she could not bear to see a scissor of any kind. The sensation of having her hair cut would be too dreadful. In the street she held his hand tightly. He was very careful with her. They walked around the small streets, up and down the main shopping area, through the pedestrian walks. Sometimes she clung to his arm, a small woman with a large belly, feeling her weight, knowing with every step that something was wrong with the child.

'What am I going to do, Tage?'

'What about, Lois?'

'With another child.'

'Feed it. It is mine.'

'You don't know what I am talking about.'

'Tell me, then, Lois.'

Along the cathedral walk, the wind blew some small leaves around in a circle, the first leaves of the autumn.

'What about the baby?'

'Nothing.'

'Nothing, Lois?'

'Tage, this is your first baby, this is my sixth. This time it may be so difficult for me.'

'I know that. But why do you think so now?'

'I don't know. I don't know myself.'

'Don't you know what is wrong? Is it a medical problem? We can get a better doctor.'

'It's not that, Tage. Perhaps the problem is in my head and nowhere else. I hope so, anyway.'

'I see. It's me, isn't it? It's because I am here with you.'

'No, Tage. You are good for me now.'

'I am very fond of you, Lois. I do not want to see anything happen to you.'

'Thankyou.'

'How much longer will it be?'

'I don't know. I don't know. Three more weeks, they say, but it will be longer.' She looked hard at him.

'I'm sorry, Lois. I didn't know it was like this. For other people it seems so easy, so happy a time. I thought it would be like that for us too. I didn't know.'

'I'll have to lie down.'

Pulling him towards the taxis now.

They went home again. The streets all blending into one. Tage wrestling with the door key. Up the stairs and into my bed. Breathing too heavily. No fresh air anywhere in this town. Tage bringing her a glass of water. She said she did not care about anything, just so long as she could go on living, because she was to outlive her boys, and they must have a chance to live. He went downstairs and telephoned the doctor. Then he came upstairs again and held her hand, but he was shaking too much and had to let go. She sat up and, one by one, took off her clothes. A thin woman even now, going a little grey, with a very large belly. What would happen to her? Tage shutting his eyes firmly. How would he live without her, with all those children? If he lost his own? If that one was lost? Hands over his head, elbows on his knees. Don't get sick and die, Lois, I would never live again.

'I've called the doctor. You may be going into labour. Are you? Why do you look like that? You have gone red and white and blue. What has happened? What has gone wrong?'

'Leave me.'

Under her gaze. Her eyes round.

'Let me help you. You look ill. Please lie down. The doctor will be here soon. Don't worry, Lois. Hold on.'

'My fingers are going prickly.'

'I'm sure it is nothing. The doctor will be here soon. A man doesn't know what to do in a situation like this. This is different from horses and cows.'

'Oh blimey!'

'What is it?'

'It hurts. I want to get on my knees and crawl about.'

'Well go on then. Get up.'

Lois pulling herself up, turning over to rock to and fro on hands and knees.

'Any better?'

'Much better, Tage.'

'Let's get you off the bed. You look silly there, with the doctor coming. Please, Lois. You can't stay there. The doctor will think you are really peculiar and take you away. I don't know what to do about this. Please, Lois. You don't look right there. You might fall off the bed.'

Her fingers clutching the side of the bed. Dump me in the bathroom and leave me alone.

'Lois, put some clothes on. You may have to go to the hospital.'

She put her head down at the edge of the bed, and slowly, slowly, the tears began to trickle down her face onto her upper lip, where they dripped into the carpet on the floor. And she cried soundlessly, hopelessly, while Tage bustled around downstairs, opening a can of beer, poking his head out of the door to watch for the doctor's car, which would never come. There was but one doctor who would be welcome now, and he was far away across the valley full of houses, behind high walls, his white coat behind the door. He was half recumbent on the chair with its wooden arms, thinking of Lois while a young nurse threaded her thin legs through the arms of the chair, and sat well down into his lap, facing him. A feat attempted only in youth.

'Tage?'

'Yes?'

'Tage, the pain has gone. I really feel much better now.'

'It has?'

'Oh yes. It was only the system limbering up. Like it does.'

'Really?'

'Yes, it does that.'

'What a relief, but are you sure?'

'Cancel the doctor, Tage.'

'Cancel?'

'Yes please, Tage. It will be alright now.'

'Lois, you always make a fool of me.'

'Please, Tage. I'm not well enough. I did not do it on purpose.'

'I think you do. You do it to frighten me. To make attention on yourself.'

'Please, Tage, don't sulk now.'

'Sulk? Me sulk? You sulk. Always you sulk.'

'Oh God, Tage, your English goes to pot when you get upset.'

'So what? What does it matter to you?'

'It's as well to know that your English goes to pot when you get upset.'

'I wonder if we will ever be happy again. I wonder if you will ever be my wife.'

'Good God, Tage. What is this?'

'The baby will come out. And then we will have to live together properly again. I won't have to look after you and be worried about you all the time. I will be able to give time to my own affairs. I have a life too. If I have to live here, I need to know that we can live together. We ought to be in Sweden. I don't like it here. I want to go home and take you with me. It is only right. It is only fair for me. I want our child to grow up with my mother in Sweden. Other wives go home with their husband. You just want to stay here in this cheap house. Why do you do that?'

'Security, Tage. The sameness of it all. Even with your furniture.'

'I felt so bad an hour ago with your rocking around on the bed. It was terrible. I felt so guilty. As though it was all my fault, as though I should never have married you and took you away from something.'

'You did, Tage. You should never have married me. I am poison to decent people like you.'

'Why are you telling me?'

'My time is coming. I want to tell you. To comfort you.'

'Well this is no comfort, Lois.'

'Yes, I know.'

'I just wanted my own children. I know you already had lots of children, but I thought we could start again, and I did not care if you did not have any for me. I wanted you because you did not want me. And I did not have any experience of the English. Why are you laughing?'

'I'm just thinking of what you say. You can be very funny, Tage. And ironical.'

Tage, offended, turning away.

'Tage, did you really think that I might not have any more children?'

'I did not think about it too much. I thought it might not be fair.'

'And did you want your own children very much?'

'Well, of course, but it was you I married.'

'I knew it. I feel very honoured, Tage. You don't know how you have bucked me up.'

'Really? I don't understand.'

'You're not meant to understand. It's just that I thought otherwise of you. Sometimes.'

'I don't know what to think of you.'

'Put your arms around me, Tage.'

'What?'

'It's easy. Look.'

'No, you are so big.'

'I am thinking of England, Tage.'

'Your homeland.'

'No. Just an expression at such times.'

'That must explain the British Empire, Lois.'

'Yes, I see that, dear. Tage, a woman needs a man to put his arms around her, however insincere and temporary. That is the way of things. Wives know about this sort of thing. Davey was putting his arms around me to the end, and that was the right thing to do, too. Davey was alright, really. Cooking and cleaning for him all the time while he was out all day. I couldn't stand him in the kitchen, you know. Just like you. But you do a lot of work in the house now. Very helpful, Tage. But not right, really. I should be doing it really. Perhaps if you had been a bit more cold towards me. Your love envelops me, you see. It strangles me. It drowns me. Love is like water, you know. It drowns people.'

'When I was six I was nearly drowned in the lake.'

'I know, Tage.'

'I was fishing alone in November.'

'Your mother told me.'

'I should not have gone there but boys do that.'

'And you got excited and walked to one side of the boat, something you had never done before, although you were practically born in a boat. And your mother came running for no reason as though a spirit was behind her with a stick. Something drove her to you.'

'Oh, she told you.'

'That is a mother's instinct. That is love.'

'For God's sake, Lois. Leave me something. Leave me some story to tell.'

'Yes, Tage, I will.'

These pleasantries. My memory makes me suffer. His fills him with a sort of pride. All the love that I have ever had. Davey's arms around me. Locked with Tage in a battle which cannot be won except by love. And love is missing here. His arms like concrete. Oh love is not like the water he nearly drowned in. No, it flows freely and digs channels wherever it finds its way, wherever the unyielding rock is weak. It is so gentle and soft and amenable, and takes any shape circumstances require. And it is devastating when one day it bursts through the side of the mountain. It sweeps everything out of the way. So keep building it up, Tage, small favour upon small favour, and finally you will win me: just when all I want is a new start, another stab at it. Oh, it is all so unjust. Yes, I shall remember this when I am suffering. Doctor David John's diffidence. His bewilderment. What to do now? No tickling and rolling over and over in the grass. No. The impedimenta of living rooms, institutional chairs, the knick-knacks which hold their history and ours. These are the tiny threads that bind us to our routines. Nothing more. Turn down an empty glass. Only the sacrum remains. And at the end of time, what will be left to reconstruct? Marjorie wobbling towards the grateful Arab on her high heels. The Arab who adores her pale, blooming, mature flesh, with its light blue veins. A succulent body, almost unused, nurtured in the country, which has borne no children. Rare, wonderfully enticing. Of course, of course. It was inevitable, Marjorie. He would have bought me in a job lot to serve the tea to the servants and wring out the rags at the street door. But you he would have paid a good price for, you, a pearl of price. You belonged in the crate with the carpets, Marjorie. Where are you now? Are you suffering a late pregnancy, are you to face the scrutiny of a mother-in-law perhaps six or seven years older than you, who was engaged at birth, married at nine and was conceiving, dead and buried by twelve? She will have no understanding of your agony, Marjorie, five of her twelve sons already dead in struggles you have never imagined. She will wonder what on earth is wrong with you, you who are greatly privileged, and why you cry all day and sit in the heat of the sun, why you pat the cur on the head yet kick the clean stones in the wilderness which were created for your worship of her God. And her son, who seemed so self-assured at Heathrow, herding you and the suitcases on the plane, will now seem a stranger, bowed under with worry and fear, will look at you sideways, will sigh a lot, and finally, after many many trials, will ask somebody else to put you on that wonderful plane back to Blighty. And you won't even notice what has happened to you. Ah, but Penaluna won't be there now with his van to pick you up at the station. Penaluna's van will be a permanent history, fixed, formulated, sprawling on a pin, brought out at weak moments as a tearful anecdote for uncomprehending friends of a new world.

Lois' hands dug into the sheets. I may be wrong, I may be wrong. I hope I am. The pain came again, a long needle of brilliant light inside Lois. Tell me about the cords that bind us, Tage. That make me suffer for my friend from Toldhu Close, who went away and will never be seen hereabouts again. At least in her old form. Let this life tear itself away from me before it overwhelms me. I am not ready for this. I sat upon the shore fishing, the arid plain behind me. The nymphs are departed . . .

CHAPTER 10

Coming out of the front door with Tage. In one's finest maternity outfit, feeling very well, all the sickness and false starts of the last few days entirely forgotten on this lovely summer evening. Oh happy day, the heavy flowers of late summer are in bloom in the garden, I see. The wild scent of honeysuckle in the hedgerow overwhelming the garage and me. Did the builder who cut down your beeches and made your squirrels homeless forget himself with regard to this honeysuckle and this hedgerow? Let's see what we have in the freezer in the garage, Tage. Plenty of meat and ice-cream for you all during my sojourn in the hospital ~ when the time comes. Walking down to town and getting a taxi from there to whatever restaurant I fancy. Back home at ten thirty or eleven for a warm bath and a cuddle up to my nice warm Tage, my husband, my chosen.

'Good evening, dear sir, dear madam.'

A yes, good evening. Here we are now in the same restaurant with the pink chairs.

'How did you know about this restaurant, Lois? Good menu. Try the scampi.'

Irradiated seafood, passed through strange, occult rays for our delight. How do I know about this restaurant? Ah. My life turns ever around, Tage, but the same wheel carries me. And every second the burden of momentum gets heavier.

'Have a piece of steak, Lois. Good for your blood.'

Blood for blood. An eye for a sheep's eye. 'Yes, a matter of belief.'

'What?'

'It's a matter of personal belief, Tage. Some very healthy people cannot stand to eat any meat at all. Others eat their own afterbirth. In fact both sorts are like to do the same. I think I'll have a nut salad, dear. If they have one.'

'Cornwall's at its best this time of year, Lois.'

'For the tourist. Grand evenings.'

'If you were not so big I would take you to Land's End to see the sunset after our meal.'

'I know you would, Tage.'

'It will be alright, Lois. I know it will be alright.' Taking her hand.

Conversation. The art of conversation. Is there any hope of reconciliation before I pronounce you disenfranchised? No, Your Honour. He still has no conversation, and I . . .

Into my gloom. To the bottom of my pool. Why have I come here, to the menu with the pick and shovel motif? Why have I conned Tage into coming here with me? Not for nothing, no. To live in the shadow of a memory. To be fortified. The tonic of a memory. No. Because memory is slippery, as somebody has said before, and time . . . ah, time. 'Time is a great healer', said that fool Robins over his sherry glass, projecting his deepest thoughts across space and into the world by telex that very morning, regarding the drawing of a fur coat for his wife. You have to live through this, Lois. You can't sleep it away, although you can avoid most hours when others are awake. Are the walnuts polished with silicone, waitress? Perhaps I won't have the slimmer's salad after all.

Tage's rumbling stomach. This is not the waitress of heretofore, when Doctor David John stared back at me amidst the forest of these tables and chairs, attentive, happy, and wary, so wary. He had a lot to lose, and the time was not right. Me expecting Tage's baby very soon, the nurses back at the hospital amenable, sterile, gentle even. Pushed his meat to the side of the plate. Nervous.

Across from here, on that very table, Doctor David John pressed my knee for an instant before apologising. Significance? There is no significance in anything. Tage is here with me as before. He was present in the ether on that very night. I carry him around with me. His blood runs in my infant's body, not separated from me yet. That table is not *that* table. They have had a banquet here since that night, and all the tables have been moved. Polished, moved around. His fingerprint has gone from that table. But our existence, what we have done and said on a different day, in a different mood, is all we have to go on. If I were to ask the overwhelming question, and then make the overwhelming decision to go, to look for you, David John, out of context, as the world has it, what thing could then be said that might overturn a universe that accommodates both you and me, but not together? Why do it? Because you said I was lovely?

These clerks on their anniversary night out. Another notch in the stake. Why do it, why celebrate, why remember a day in the year, roughly corresponding to this one, when it rained or it shone on Bognor or Brighton or granny's back yard? What are the roots that clutch to that stony earth? What is the meaning of those fresh flowers in the photograph? What are those pressed flowers in the album? To keep a memory green. Of the darkening green. Leave me alone with my dry thoughts. Perhaps I am going mad here. But I can't be. Tage is enjoying himself so much. And his enjoyment of life leeches upon my soul, and reminds me of my solitude which, perhaps in the midst of this, and even because of this I can preserve still. In my own brand of emptiness.

Tage won me and was glad. Far and away the best husband for me. Accommodating to all my weariness, my disenchantment, my bad temper, my nastiness and badness. The canker in his rose bed. Even though I was a third class citizen and he had to appease his mother, night and day, in order to have me.

That girl of twenty there, celebrating her third anniversary with the clerk from Gold's the estate agents. Too much by way of commission and salary for these types. How different it might have been for her if he had not given in to the pressure of respectability, of family, of the threads that bind even the low: particularly the low. What are those threads? Is that the knowledge my overturned mind is after? What makes the lecher a family man? What now gives Davey's wife the power that keeps him away from us? No. What restricts Davey so that he cannot and dare not? That restraint is in his mind alone. Not in hers. She can only be grateful it is firmly in place. That teasy, nervous woman. That bitch. That bastard. To exclude my children from their father. He does it himself, Lois. He has legs. He can come to the children. But he tells himself things, things that make him feel easier about it all. In Memoriam, Davey, we may never see you again until your funeral.

And the congregation shall sing, 'There will be a bright tomorrow.' And Tage, holding on to my arm, will enjoy the hope therein, the community singing. And the angels will enjoy the justice of it. Oh come, Lois: even God proposed to leave the judgement until the end of the story.

What was it Grandma Davey used to say? 'The end of the story has not been told yet. Wait for the end of the story.'

But I might outwait my time. Like the Quakers, who thought until their hands went brown, and went away, and closed their meeting houses.

Ah, but you do not know the power of thought, my precious. I must go back to Davey. I am looking for Davey in all of this. Doctor David John is a dalliance in the mind. David John is without significance. He has no history with us. Davey has significance. Yes, and if I go to Davey, what will it be but a short interview in the damp front room which once was mine? With my old possessiveness coming up to choke me. Will I leave with a pocketful of my old ornaments? The old racehorse of cracked china? Valueless, meaningless to her, his bitch. All I had left of my mother. Will she scream at me again, or will she stand, wiping her hands on her pinafore, the alien lady who took the prize and lost the world. My grandfather lives in Davey. He begins to develop the old man's stoop. I see him hold a stick as Grandfather Davey did. I know what he thinks. His new wife can only dream what he thinks. She can only imagine. And Davey would laugh, enjoying the battle. And he would put us both across the table if he had the sense. But Davey never did have much sense. So he had to choose, and chose only to stay and feed the cattle, as he has done for a thousand years.

'I said, Lois, will you have a glass of wine? Lois.'

Tage's face thrust forward. Not amused. A silly smile has frozen on my face and I did not know it.

'Sorry, Tage, I wasn't listening.'

'Wine, Lois. Will you have the wine?'

'Sorry, Tage, I can't drink it. I will have to have the orange juice again.'

'And the lady will have an orange juice. Please.'

'I can't take wine, Tage, you know that.'

'Yes, Lois.'

Oh, this is awful. If Doctor John were to come here with his friends and see us and walk up to us. Tage would know. He knows now that there is some significance in this damned place for me. What shall I do now?

No conversation. Tage has no conversation in any language. 'Look, there's a bird,' and other inanities. I wanted to kill Davey that time I saw them in the supermarket and I went up to her. There were two doughnuts at the top of the trolley. Things he would never allow me to buy. Things I had to bake myself. Everything homely and home cooking in the damned Aga. And there she was in the supermarket discussing his dinner with him. Something which I could never do. I could have served a heap of hay and he would have eaten it. This is bitterness. She had the knack with him and I did not.

Or she placed priorities on things I did not. She controls him and I do not.

'Talk to me, Lois. This is becoming a bore. You asked me to take you out to dinner. Please Lois.'

If only you did not plead with me so much. If only you were as before. Violent, unpredictable. Masculine.

'Oh, Lois.'

Grasp the nettle. Pull it up and throw it out of the garden before it becomes deep rooted. A weed left today is a wilderness next year. But I could not nag him as she does. I could not make him eat doughnuts from a supermarket trolley. I loved him so much. I admit it now. To myself. Sitting here in this restaurant which I came to only to admit to myself my weakness for Doctor David John: to indulge myself a little in my weakness.

'I love you, Lois.'

'I love you, Tage.' I have to.

No hope. Words drip like honey from the tongue. Meaning . . . nothing. Where, then, is the meaning? In the need to say them? In the impulse to say them? To fill the void with words which are only applicable to somebody else at this moment? And that somebody else is not the one who stood before you a thousand times before, whom you grew not to love at all, but to find a terrible restriction. A pain in the arse. And with no conversation. No: you can't judge it, then, on conversation alone. Davey was a lout. But it was meaningful. You spent meaningful years with Davey the lout. As you are not doing with Tage.

I am avoiding your eyes, Tage. I cannot look into them. They will show me my reflection. I cannot have peace when they show me my reflection. Deliver me from this evil. This thought that goes on and on. Cornered, trapped. What will become of us now? I will sort of come to love you, dear. The feeling is so important to women. The form is so important to men. And what if Davey should die some afternoon, the rain falling on the autumn stubble, pinned under that rampant old tractor? Will I not say that I should have been there, and would have been there, were it not for her? Don't I mean for him? For me?

Tage making for the door. I don't blame you, Tage. I am a menace. I am no company for you tonight. I am a waste of dinner money.

Tage slamming the taxi door, sitting in his own corner of the car. I have offended Tage.

Come to me, my sweet.

'When this baby is out, I will, Tage.'

CHAPTER 11

A bitter pill to swallow. Holding on to the cup with both hands. I can't take these iron pills. I think they will kill me. I have a feeling about them. I can't take the vitamin pills. I don't want them. I know what my blood must be like. But I don't want them. Not if I shall go to an early grave instead. I can't. I don't want them. Leave me alone. I don't want them. They will poison me. This is a worry. Stop hurting me, Tage. Stop persecuting me.

'Could I have hot water instead, Tage?'

'Hot water? To drink pills?'

Please Tage. Go downstairs so that I can make a hole in the quilt and shove the tablets in there. Lie on my back, though it feels strange. The fingers of my left hand are tingling. Always the same lately. Do I have circulatory problems? I think so. I am afraid so. Oh, now, why me, why me?

Tage sat down on the wicker chair beside the bed and took her hand in his. It had about it a frailty which touched him deeply. Lois, who was always so strong, was now ailing; and he had it on the best authority, there was nothing wrong with the woman. Was it to insult him? To wear him down? So that she could have her way, win this everlasting battle for once and for all?

He looked at her coldly.

'I feel ill, Tage.'

Tage disbelieving.

'I'm ill, Tage. There is something wrong with the baby.'

'Lois, there is nothing wrong with the baby. You have had all the tests it is possible to have. There is nothing wrong.'

'Except in my head.'

'Except in your head.'

'Is that true?'

'Yes, Lois, that is truth.'

'Truth.'

'Lois, it doesn't work any more. Get out of the bed and walk around. There is nothing wrong with you. I know it. You know it. The doctor, he knows it. Give me rest, Lois. Give me peace. There is nothing wrong with you. Not now, not never. Lois.'

Not ever. Not ever.

'Please don't raise your voice, Tage, you frighten me.'

'Nothing frightens you, Lois, except not having everything the way you want it.'

'You are upsetting me, Tage. Don't upset me any more.'

'Lois, you are not able to be upset. You have never been upset. You have never been ill. You have never cared what I thought about you or your illness.'

'You'll remember that when I am gone, Tage. You'll remember every word of it. My ghost will remind you, even in Flen. Every morning you will wake up, and for an instant everything will be alright. Then you will remember. Lois is gone. And you said she was not ill.'

'I am going back to Flen, Lois, after the baby is born. I will wait until then.'

'Yes, I thought I was feeling ill. You will deny paternity as well, for good measure, will you? That's typical, isn't it. You get me pregnant, ruin my life, give me a kid that I didn't want, your one and only son and heir, after taking me away from a perfectly decent and happy life with a Cornishman, you blackmail me into living with you in some stinking foreign country, you put my life at risk and then you announce that you are going home. Well sod you, Tage. Piss off. I'll fetch for myself. Where are my boys? They know how to look after their mother.'

Tage taken aback by the force of her feeling, so adequately expressed. He knew, of course, had always known she was like this. A fake. No good. As his mother had told him.

Tage made up his mind.

'I am going back to Flen. I am going back to my farm. I don't care what you do. I will pay the bills.'

'Don't bother.'

'Oh yes, Lois. It was my mistake.'

'Oh shut up, shut up. I am going to be sick.'

'You are not sick. Do you understand me? You are only sick in the head.'

'Stop it, Tage.'

'So, you are going to be sick, then. Be sick.'

Lois beginning to weep.

'Come on, Lois, if you are going to be sick.'

'Leave me alone, Tage. Please.'

'Come on, Lois, come on.'

'I'm ill, Tage. Leave me alone.'

'No no, come on, Lois. I am here to help you be sick.'

'Tage, the truth is this, I want to be left alone. Leave me alone. I don't want to be here, I don't want you here, I want to be left alone to die. I am going to die, anyway. You punched me when I was just a few weeks pregnant. You didn't know. But you made me ill then. I know what it is. Tage, don't hurt me any more. Just leave me alone to die. Please, Tage. Leave me alone.'

'Lois, you are driving me mad too. We can't both stay in the house and repeat the same things over and over.'

Lois looking frightened. Her eyes pink. Her face blue. Tage had not noticed that before.

'I'm sick, Tage. I know I have had all the tests, but I know something is wrong. No, it is not your fault. It is my fault, perhaps. But there is something. Perhaps it is in my mind. I ought not to be agitated like this at this stage. Surely that is evidence enough that I am not well. Surely. Don't leave me at this point. The children don't know what is wrong and they can't cope with the young ones. I can't cope with the young ones either. Please, Tage.'

'Shut up, Lois.'

'I see.'

'You have said enough, Lois.'

'I see.'

He stood up slowly, the wicker chair creaking. He stood looking out of the window. A cold, unremarkable moon stared in at him.

'Are you going out, Tage?'

'Yes.'

He walked out of the room and down the stairs. She heard the front door slam.

'At least all the boys are indoors and the baby is asleep.'

'Get out of my bedroom, all of you. Get out. Get out. Paul, take them out of here.'

'You're really sick, mum.'

'Yes, Andrew, I think I really am sick. I think I really am.'

'Is it our fault, mum?'

'Go away, please. Don't make me cry in front of the young ones.'

'We really are sorry, mum. Are you going to die?'

'I can't tell you anything, Paul, but no, I am not going to die. I am just going to have a baby, that's all. It won't be long now.'

They trooped down the stairs, silently, feet dragging all the way. I felt sorry, so very sorry. And weary of it all.

'Stay away from me, children. Stay away from me, O shadow which follows me around mercilessly. Let me have my rosy sunsets of autumn. They cost me nothing, nothing at all. Tage can't live in this country: no-one can live in this country. Give me the strength to endure. Give me the strength. I stood at the gate of the year and . . . I said to the man who stood at the gate of the year . . . Why do I have to suffer this, do you suppose? The sunsets soon are gone. Study, work, study, work with your hands, my little ones. Life is soon over.

It is as well to rub the skin off your hands. That is what they are for. It will soon fall off your bones.'

'Can I come in, mum?' The hurt and pain and half anger behind the eyes. You suffer for your mother, my dear one. Come on in, then, and sit on my bed.

'The tapes are just £1.50, mum. I really would like one.'

'I have sat here, Paul, day after day after day. I have been so absorbed in my own troubles I haven't even noticed how you are or even who you are.'

'O mum, please don't be upset.'

'Quiet, Paul, the others will hear you.'

'Please mum, please don't be upset.'

'For Christ's sake, Paul, what did I just tell you? I don't want the little ones to hear you. They will be up here again. They haven't had any childhood as it is.'

'When will the baby come, mum?'

'Soon. I am resting now. It will be soon.'

'How do you know?'

'There's a tremendous pressure for weeks, and then it all eases and becomes lighter. Then I get very busy and agitated. Then, there is a sort of silence inside me, like waiting for the time. And then the time comes. The baby is mine then, delivered into the world. There is no time like that. I love you all, Paul. I remember you all, the hour you were born, everything about you. Give me my novel, Paul.'

'Where?'

'On the floor there.'

'Mum, talk to me, like when I was the only one and you used to talk to me all the time. I remember it, mum, before Andrew was born and took my place. Honestly. I know you say that's impossible, but I do remember. I do remember.'

'I think that's impossible, my darling one.'

'I do remember.'

'Maybe so, maybe so. What does it matter now, Paul? You are the oldest, anyway, my firstborn. Nothing can alter that, now, can it?'

'No mum.'

'I put five pounds in your savings book the other day. Five pounds for each of you. Not much, but five each.'

'OK. Thanks, mum.'

'I'll do all I can for you all, but there are so many of you now. But I gave you life. That is all that matters. And you are perfect, all of you.'

'It's OK mum, we never want anything while we have you and Tage.'

'Is that a tear I see in your eye?'

'No.'

Lois with her arm around her boy's shoulders, leaning outwards from the bed. Whatever will they think of women when they grow? What will they think of their own wives, my daughters? It won't be long, it won't be long now. We are all caught in time. Especially me. I am caught in time more than most, at the moment. Or rather, aware of all that, at the moment. To hell with it.

Where is Tage now? How far down the street? The lamplight on him. Drinking in a teenage bar for dear life. Ordering another. Watching the fake gas fire flicker. A cunning fire. Attracted to the crossed legs and the iced makeup in the corner. Neapolitan. Affecting the casual, the Viking working on the situation. It won't take him long now. Clutching the soles of dirty feet in soiled hands. He had a way with him, that American, looking over the rooftops. They all had a left bank education, those post-war poets. Lloyds, in his case. Ha ha. A joke for myself. And Ted Hughes went on the O Level syllabus.

But now, let us concentrate the mind. After the event, after the event we shall go on picnics. We shall smooth out the oilcloth and we shall buy some nice blue and white plastic plates, and one of those expensive straw baskets, and we shall be going on picnics. The sort of things that people try to do when they think they are trying to make the best of things and the old man gets a hernia trying to carry the boat down the coastal footpath to the isolated creek. Tee hee. Then again, I shall take up the knitting again. Oh yes, Aran sweaters all round, my dears. One for each. Knitting up a whole flock of sheep. With enthusiasm. Being the wife, don't you know.

'Try your arm in this sleeve, dear.'

'Oh very nice, mum,' and no trace of sarcasm.

'Try your neck in here, Tage.'

'Oh very nice, darling. You are a clever wife. A wife is worth a hundred secretaries I always say. Worth her weight in gold.'

'Abraham's wives wore their weight in gold, I expect, dear.'

'Your diamond is one point five carats.'

'Carrots, yes.'

'Well, there you are then.'

'Yup. There I am then.'

'Bigger diamonds are not much use for jewellery.'

'Nope. Not much use at all. My hands are going, anyway. You need new hands for a ring job.'

'Are you being vulgar, Lois?'

'Nope. You don't need many carrots, not in this street.'

Ah, happy days. Happy, bantering days. Tell you what I used to like, though, when I was only nine years old or thereabouts. I used to like the old fair-isle patterns. Lovely. I could work on those forever. I used to listen to the radio with Mother. The afternoon play. It was always good then. Sometimes a detective story, sometimes a story with social interest. Sometimes a mystery. And the library in Smith's bookshop. All gone. All gone. Isn't Tage an oaf?

Kissing my boy on the ear. I love him so. But not that much. There always has to be a way out. There always has to be a way out.

Out into the breeze. The heather colours of the fair-isle patterns, and the sheep and the moorland of yesteryear. Before the Council schemes took over the derelict land. I tell you, they cannot change us. They cannot get into our very soul. I tell you, we will remain. I'll tell you how. You see how the gorse has colonised the banks. It will move forward onto the grass and choke it out. The heather will move back in and choke it all out. And when the tall trees, the deciduous trees find out what is there, under the soil, they will die, my friend. And the rain will wash away the soil. As the rain washed away the very burrows that were the last testament of labouring men on that hillside. And that is how you and I will survive. We are adapted and they are not. Time will tell. Time. What is the use of time if it cannot say anything? Listen to what it tries to tell you. But, you say, your brother is a half-breed. Will he half survive, then?

Tage's suede boot at the door. Lois upstairs, reading her novel. He won't be going out any more this evening, then. Peace, peace, give us all peace. Dear Jesus, come and sit beside me. Really must write a little letter to dear old Marjorie, you know. O my dear old friend, don't die in London. So many things to die of. So many things people are heir to. Don't die, Marjorie. Why do I say that, now? Do you think that Tage or one of the boys will make some soup for me? With some bread? Did I have toast for breakfast today? Was I alive yesterday as usual? Stay calm and quiet. Nobody can hurt you now. Not quite now. Is this guilt or bad nerves? Or both or nothing?

'Lois.'

'There he was at the edge of the bed, but quiet now and far distant, his anger gone. Just a frightened man. Afraid of his wife, afraid of life.

'Open up again, Tage.'

'What?'

'You're all closed in. There is a way. By opening up.'

'What?'

'By saying yes to the universe.'

'You're nuts. You've gone over the top.'

'No. It isn't that. You see, I have discovered a lot of things from my vantage point. You wouldn't understand. I know what I mean, anyway. Do you know that you suffer from a very stiff neck?'

'What do you mean by that?'

'Your neck is stiff.'

'And that is all?'

'Unfortunately, yes, dear Tage.'

'Yes.'

'Yes.'

'The most interesting thing that ever happened to me was getting married to an English, no, a Cornish lady.'

'Yes, you poor devil. I'm sorry about that.'

Almost pleasure in the air now. Almost good humour, laughter, fun. Life is good when you have fun. Marriage is fun when you have fun. We all like it that way. The noose slackens. Build a garage, tear down a wall, search out the damp. That's the way. Get busy. Life is very nice when one is nice, working for one's family. Even for Davey's family. Good old Tage. Easily controlled by a bad temper, like most men. Well, here we are, then, all friendly.

'A little salmon and toast?'

'Oo yes, Tage, with some butter.'

'I will bring it up to you.'

'And then I will bring it up, tee hee.'

'What?'

'Never mind, my darling. Are the kids watching the TV? Yes, of course they are. What else, now?'

'O Lois, they are all right. They are all right.'

You had better believe it, chum.

'We won't be having a divorce, then, Tage? I thought we would, what with you going off out all the time. Never mind, dear I don't believe in divorce either. Not at all. Most liberating. Means we can hack each other's egos to pieces with impunity until the grave, yes? Yes.'

Tage stood by the window. His hands gripped the narrow window ledge. Humph. In labour, one gripped the window ledge a damn sight harder than that.

'Now, that is not very fair again, Lois. I don't like to hear you say that again, Lois.'

Tage's hand gripped the handle of the window, and broke it off, snap. He was as surprised as Lois.

'Ploughboy's hands again, Tage. I think I'll go to sleep. You wreck the place all the time. Another job for Penaluna to do.'

Tage stomped down the stairs, holding the window handle. Lois heard him throw it down. She heard him go out and pull up the door of the garage.

'O Tage, Tage, what are you doing now? You are wrecking my damned house. Why can't you leave us alone?'

'Mummy, Tage's gone into the garage with a piece of the window.' Intelligent Paul at the top of the stairs.

'It's alright, Paul. He knows what he's doing. Honestly.'

'Yes, but . . .'

'It's alright, Paul. Really it is.'

'You smell nice, mum.'

Yes, it's my Evening in Probus. Very nice.

My universe is controlled from my bed. Even in bed they all come to me. Mum this, mum that. They are only males.

What can I do for them? I don't even feed them now. And my present marriage depends on that. Yes, depends.

> *My darling Marjorie,*
>
> *Here I am in my bed enjoying myself. I am very disciplined, as you may imagine. I have three meals a day, light meals, which Tage and the children prepare for me. Then I go for a little stroll to the toilet. Very good for my pregnancy. I am waiting. This is the final trimester, or term, as we used to call it in school. I don't feel at all desperate, dear, no not at all. I do all my nice deep breathing silly exercises, like people do. Good for me. I have a good time nearly all day. For one thing, guess what? I have a little tape recorder and I practice not one, not two, not three but four different languages during the day. Swedish, of course, also Danish, German and French for a complete change. Unfortunately, Tage is not very patient with my attempts at his language so we stick to English, which he thinks he knows very well. But I do keep catching him out, tee hee. Old Tage keeps pulling the house apart. This very evening he stretched his hand out in a dramatic gesture and pulled the catch off the window, but at least he didn't stuff his fist through it. I still love it here in Toldhu. I don't see much of Penaluna, but I shall be needing him soon to do a few jobs around the house if Tage stays here much longer. I think he will be staying, actually. But where are you? Are you still in London? Or have you gone up north or something like that? Not to the Home Counties, I trust? Something tells me you will be back here before long. They always come back, the*

117

Cornish. Quite adventurous, really, driven out by Granny or the Old Man, but they always come back. Well, nowhere else has any meaning or makes any sense, you see, not for the Cornish. Don't have to tell you, though, do I?

What do you reckon, then? Will it be a boy or a girl? Another boy, of course. I only have boys, though that's the fault of the man, so perhaps it will all be different with Tage the Viking man. Do you think I should give up having children after this? Course you do. Whatever, this will be my last, mate, don't ever doubt it. Well, this one is killing me. I have had all sorts of strange feelings, not good at all, during this pregnancy. Not good at all. Perhaps now, do you think that every man's children feel different in the womb? The reason why I mention it is that Davey's all felt the same. Sort of. If you know what I mean. Nope: guess you don't know what I mean. Ah well, there we are, then, each of us trapped in our misery. Or not, as the case may be. You know, Marjorie, the one thing I should like to take up again is, guess what, the piano. Yes, Marjorie, the piano. Not as when I was teaching, no, when I was a kid growing up. And did you know that nowadays, a little keyboard can sound like a Steinway? Well, I would say of course that after a while it wouldn't sound like one to you, because you'd be playing it rain and shine, summer and winter and it would sound the same. You know, no shrinking of the wood, no rusting of the wire. No wearing of the felts. Well you know, moaning about the piano and having it tuned were such important things to people. A seasonal thing, you know, like rheumatics. Just like rheumatics, Marjorie. It's like using a typewriter. You have to change the ribbon sometimes. It's no good if the thing goes on and on like a computer printer. Oh never mind, Marjorie. How are you in dear old London now? Having a good time, I expect, I hope. Marjorie, for God's sake be careful. I worry about you. There might be a problem if you ignore all the signs. City life: Babylon, dear. I miss you, my dear. I miss you, now.

Haven't seen anybody, you know, none of the old friends. Well, they were no friends to us, were they? What about the Vigus twins, then? Never thought much of them, before or after. Well, so there we go, then. Marjorie, I'm bored, so very bored. And miserable. That's the fact of it. I thought I would be alright, but I'm not. I can't say I love it here in the Close, because I don't. I don't exactly hate it here, either. But I don't like it here, especially without you. How are the children? Alright, I suppose. I don't see much of them lately. I spend all of the time in bed, you know. Yes, in bed. Silly, isn't it. Still, there we are, then. Everybody is different. I've had enough. That's the fact of it, old girl. I don't think I will get away from this in one piece. I feel hemmed in. Hemmed in. Hemmed in. Nobody is going to rescue me. It will just have to happen on its own. One day I will see a light and go for it. So they say. Remember how you felt, sweetheart? That's the way I feel now. Exactly so. When it rains, it comes at you sideways. But I don't like this grey weather. Like Leicester, only cold.

119

Midsummer, eh? Who would believe it? Ever been to the wax museum or the National Gallery? There were pictures I used to go and stare at every time I went to London, and then, when they had the cheek to move them around I got highly offended. Associations, you see. There was a Gainsborough. I had to go and see it. And there was a Last Supper. I saw it again in a junk shop in Redruth for £30, with peeling edges. I had to have it, but somebody else did. An inferior copy, anyway, but it would have done me. Flowing robes, the sense of an ending. You know. Animation suspended in the picture. You could eat your tinned pilchards and salad and look at that all day. That's what I say, old dear. Remember when Jimmy Keyes killed Barry? What a night that was. There aren't any fights like that any more, you know. The yobs with their green hair have no idea, my darling. No idea at all. I came out of Fish Cross the other day, clutching my handbag. There were two of them with one knife and a girl. Didn't know which was the weapon and which way was the hospital. Blood everywhere. Well, that was before my sickness, you understand. I am not sick, you know, just playing up. So Tage thinks. And he is quite right. But not in the way that he thinks he is right. Tee hee, dear. Tee hee. The way of the good wife is not the way of the world.

Well, today, I am here in my bed, writing to you for some reason, although I can't be sure where you are, or who will read this instead of you. So, there is just something I want to warn you about. There have always been diseases and there has always been trouble. But there has never been anything like this, so please don't ignore the signs of the times. Because they are indeed the signs of the times, if you see what I mean. The thing is, old Marge, I am worried about your silly remark about everybody being so generous in London. Well, nobody's generous in London, although I can see that after Cornwall London might seem a mite more friendly. But generous? Marjorie, for God's sake, is all I will say about that. Will you be coming back? I would like you to. Well I know it won't be the same for a while, what with me and the new baby, but Tage will help. And you know, I kind of miss you, old pal, old beauty. You see, I just don't feel much like living any more.

Something has gone wrong with me. And I hope not with you.

CHAPTER 12

And now, the chilly, slantwise rain of summer. But not for me the raincoat of forget-me-not blue, burgeoning nicely with the child. No, not for me, friends. Instead, in the new dressing-gown meant for the hospital. It won't be needed for a few days yet, though. The doctor has been, no not *our* darling doctor, the family doctor. And he has recommended a psychologist. Nothing as desperate as the other sort of mind doctor, but an insult, none the less. I'm not speaking to Tage. Would you?

I can see by the eyes that they are not worried about me. Just about themselves. Tage doesn't know whether he has driven me mad. Tee hee. He hasn't. I have driven myself. I like doing the driving. Doesn't everybody? You see, the thing is, they are frightened. But there is no need to be. I won't survive this child the same person. I am evolving into another. It will be obvious to any outsider. Marjorie, my mate, went away, you see. You think only men have mates. Oh no. We women have mates too, on whom we depend. Not for beer and skittles. You know, I was looking across the valley and what did I see? A reading library built by the Cornish Carnegie, old Passmore Edwards. What a man that was. If Tage could have done something, anything like that.

'I love you, Lois.'

It was that sort of rubbish that finished him.

'That is not true, Tage.'

That was what finished me.

'O come on, Lois.'

That was another one. All these things conspired to stifle creativity, everything.

'Old Q, you see, was married at eighteen, never regretted it and wrote like Stevenson. He didn't regret anything, you see.'

But Tage Af Klercker, from another planet, thought Q was an old boyfriend.

'What is all this, Lois, this Cue? I get tired of hearing about other people. You compare me with other people.'

'Q was a writer, a Cornishman. He gave English literature to the world. To University students. Thereby telling the world what to go on reading during their lives. As long as they lived. And their publishers and booksellers, and children. Culture belongs to the man who can publish.'

'I am going back to Sweden, Lois.'

'There's decisive, now.'

'You are my wife.'

'Certainly.'

'These past two years.'

'Well, of course.'

Tage's eyebrows raised. I cannot help him. I would like to, but he is from another planet. Poor dear old Tage. Life is like that. People have expectations which can never be fulfilled. There are indications along the way. Not milestones. And years are just for unravelling. If you believe in fate as well as moral man. Are both things concurrent? In a world where all things are possible, then all things take place. Can we be judged for them all? Every way, there is mystery and a trap.

'Look, Lois, I know that you are sick. I know that. But I can't be happy here in this country. In a little house. I know that I bought it for you so that you could be happy and not have to work hard if something went wrong, if you had to repair it. But all I want is to go away from here. Go home. I want you and the baby to come too. All of the children.'

'I read you, Tage.'

'What? You read me? Do you mean you understand me? What I am saying to you?'

'God is on your side, Tage. You are understood. Also by me.'

'Lois, everything we say to each other, it doesn't have any sense. We are not talking to each other properly. I know that you are sick but, well, I know you can't help it.'

'Of course I can.'

'What? You can help it, being sick. I always knew that this past few weeks. You make me very unhappy, Lois.'

'Quite.'

'I think that I should go to Sweden.'

'Yes.'

'But what will happen to you and the baby?'

'Aren't you having the baby?'

'I will telephone to my mother this evening.'

'What about your baby?'

'He will have to stay with his mother. With you.'

'Oh no, Tage. Go on, Tage. Go to Sweden. But not with me. And I won't keep your baby for you. Not me. Pity you don't have a sister who will take it. But I won't. Not me.'

'Well, Lois, let's not get things wrong. This is too serious. I should not upset you at a time like this. It will be any day now.'

'Not for me, Tage.'

'I will send you money every month.'

'Thankyou, Tage.'

'I must get away from Cornwall, Lois. You must understand. This is difficult for me.'

'That's quite funny.'

Lois laughing through tears at last. Crying with eyes shut. Handsome Lois, a mother who never did any wrong. Poor Lois. She was not a bad wife. Not like some of them. It was the hard ones who got away with it all. Not good women like Lois.

'Suppose I stay until after the baby is born, our baby, Lois.'

'Suppose you don't? What difference will that make to me?'

'It will seem different after she is born, my daughter.'

'It will, will it? Yes, I expect it will, Tage, my dear.'

'We got married. I am thinking about that.'

'Yes, the certificate of marriage.'

Tage walked away from the bed and down the stairs. Very softly. Dragging his misery behind him. It was you, Tage, who threw me down the stairs in more heady days. You it was who tied your knot with me in Sweden, in a strange place. You it was who took advantage of me beside a red barn smelling of preservative. Preservative against the damp. Your jacket on the ground. And my shoes lost in the broken corn. There are different kinds of virginity, Tage, dear Tage. And you feel now that you have met the old lag in me.

In the living room, Tage sat down with a beer. Unable to understand much of the English clever panel games. Lois heard his mind retreat from hers. The undercurrent and the low buzz had gone. When they were active, she heard them in her sleep.

I'll say this, Tage, you won't hurt me again. You can't. Don't know how or why, but you can't hurt me any more. Somehow, some way, I have worked through this, and you can't any more.

This bitterness is fruitless now. Because nothing more need be said nor done. And whatever is said and done will be alright. It won't be at all bothersome. Not like the past. Not like it was in Sweden, where I hated you and still listened for your footstep at the end of the day. Where sunset should have been. No more retreating to the bath to get out of your way, to shut out your mind trying to oppress mine. You can't do that any more, and I am free. It is not that I have shut you out. It is not that I want to be rid of you. It is that I am rid of you, dear, and the rest is not worth the candle. What we said in the registrar's office, what little I understood of it, is forgiven, is void. Not the same things, for sure, but concurrent with you and me. The Certificate is irrelevant now. We are on our own. Not from this moment, from a moment some time ago. One which I did not register then, when the moment came into being, but one which I register now. Because, Tage, I have to. This is understandable in all languages. The subject is closed in my head.

Three o'clock on this golden afternoon. Lois peeps through the window at the world outside the house. Yes, yes, there it used to be, the May dying, the cherry blossom of the wife from Glasgow, her pride, all dying. They are still out there, Lois. The people of the world, that is. Still out there. Still living, still lying, still dying.

'Bring me up a nice lemon squash, you will find it in the bottom of the fridge. Please, Paul. I'd like you to.'

'To what, mum?'

'Bring me a lemon squash. It would do me good. I want to watch the world go by, and write another letter to my friend Mrs Penaluna. And just look out across the world.'

'Well, honestly, mum.'

'I know. But that's what I really want. Go on, Paul. With a little bit of ice, but not if the ice is more than two days old. It breeds things, you know.'

'O mum, I was just going to do some homework. I have got this project to do on the beach. About fishes.'

'Don't be so damn silly, Paul. I'm not pregnant in the head, you know.'

'Oh for God's sake, mum.'

Another disgruntled male, caught out in a fib. And unco-operative, to boot. I am really not well. In a terrible condition. Now to arrange my pens and pencils on the window-sill like this. As though I were going to write to the poor old dear again. I am afraid she will die. It's not unknown amongst the

Cornish in London. I haven't seen old Penaluna at all: not at all. I'm afraid, you see. Afraid to go up there, in case another woman really has taken her place. I don't want to think of Penaluna with another woman in the house. It wouldn't be right, you see. Not right at all. I had her sofa and her old mixer and her toaster and all the rest of it. But what good has it done me now? I can hardly struggle out of the bed. It's a judgement on me. That's what it is. Dear me, yes. I will die in this place. By this window. I hate it here. Nobody walks up this way. Well, it isn't at all pretty up here, is it? The occasional bloom in spring. Like the cherry trees. But that's all. They only grow the ones which stick their branches right up in the sky and get plastered with blooms once a year. Unnatural, really. Like smallpox. I used to like the ones we had on the farm. The ones which branched out all over the place. That's what I liked. Never mind. It's different here.

Lois allowed herself to think about it. Yes, all different. Her mind crossed the valley, climbed the hill, settled on the place where the water windmill pump used to be. You could see the grey outline of the farm from there.

And, by God, it wasn't a beautiful place. It was a hateful place. There, and here. Davey never got drunk a lot. You could give him that. Only in his extreme youth, and he had lost his extreme youth by the time Lois lived with Davey. The problem was, and this was a difficulty: the times in which we live now are all wrong. Something is wrong with the pace of the life we live. And I was always one of those who could not and would not let go. I had to live with Davey in my sight, never out of sight. Even when I had better things to think about. I could never let the wild animal go in the belief that it would come back to be fed. It was one of those outrages men sometimes have to live with.

There is Peter, who drives his bus in the morning and works his disco in the evening. There he is, wiping his feet before going into the green porch. Suspended in the afternoon.

'That's a lovely house you have,' they used to say. It looked fine in the sunset, and fine in the early morning. When the weather was misty it looked fine too. It was one of those awful Cornish houses that people always thought they wanted. We kept portraits of the most obscure of the ancestors. Possibly somebody else's ancestors too. What did that matter anyway? We had some sort of idea of what we were whilst we were living together. Apart, it all changed and all faltered. Was that, I wonder, why I never liked to be apart from him for a moment? We served up stew in big, thick plates, and never thought of buying anything different to eat from. We had bowls of thin cream, which we poured over everything, like bananas and tinned peaches. We had a red alarm clock with a very big face. Whatever happened to that red alarm clock with the big face? I am going to die, aren't I, thinking about all of this now. They say you remember and remember vividly, and that things come back to you, seep into your mind unbidden. That is what they say. And is this my tragic day, now? No, I don't think so. I am not going into labour for a while yet. Not on this day.

A mini-bus going down the road. The brakes hold it back, you know. One of those things you are told by your mother. And so it is. The things you are told by your mother come to be true. Would they still come true if you were an orphan? Disoriented in the world? No, no it can't be. Remember Sally Couch? Disoriented. An orphan. But not you, dear. You came of the tribe of the legitimate. And you had no trouble becoming integrated into the world. But Sally Couch did. Oh yes.

He came upstairs with a cup of tea. Weighing her mood in his foreign mind. Twisted with domestic misery. The children laughing downstairs.

'Hello, darling.'

'Did you put sugar in this time?'

He put down the tea on the little stool beside her, a stool which she used as a bedside table. She kept her ear-rings and her small pieces of gold there, visible, tawdry, unglamorous.

'And a doughnut.'

Sitting on the bed again. Taking off his shoes, smiling. Removing his trousers. Thinking about getting into the bed. As long as men are men and Lois is Lois. I would have loved a house by the sea, on a cliff. Walks along the beach with the dog. Any old dog. I would have liked that. The starkness of the cliff and the wasteland behind it. I'm not ready for you, Tage. Very sick, or so they say. You could have a little girl in town for the present. Not me, though, not yet. Ask me again in a few days. When all of this is out. As sick as I am.

'Push off, Tage, eh?'

'Certainly, Lois.'

No good trying the pumping trick with me now. I know how you feel, sort of. It's a kind of passion to want people you can't have. Especially when you married them in a foreign place and then found you can't have anybody. That the only person you have, you ever have in this world is yourself. A self-indulgence. That's why the game's all, the pursuit's all. Those men with their mowers and their greenhouses. They don't know your sorrow and your surprise, Tage. Your surprise at never getting it quite right. Would you understand if I told you about it, Tage? Would you? I hate men, I think.

'Another tea, Tage? That was a good one.'

'Just Orange Label, the cheapest.'

'Another.'

It was a strange thing, when I was a child. Now, what was it? I used to watch Mother and Uncle drink tea and I wasn't allowed one. Well, tea is no good for the complexion and rots the stomach. I thought that tea must be the most wonderful drink in all the world. When it was no such thing. Ah well, there we are. When did Tage have his first taste of tea? And you know, that was my only sin, my only shame for goodness knows how many years. Funny, that. For goodness knows how many years. Once you got over the problem of whether anybody cared or not you realised you were allowed to drink tea for the rest of your life, rain or shine, and nobody gave a darn. That nobody cared, nor ever had done. And how kind my mother was. I thought she was an angel and nobody could ever take her place. And she was. And nobody ever did. Unlike my children and me. Who could ever for one teeny weeny minute imagine that I was perfect? Perhaps my boys do. No, I don't think so. Tee hee. No I don't think so. Put your shirt back on, Tage. It is nearly autumn. All the plants are coming up orange and yellow and blue. A sure sign. Of all the girls in the school, Marjorie was the first to grow things: hairs, bits of flesh, the stuff that counts. I didn't count. But they went for me, the boys. For some reason. When Marjorie added her weight to the whole issue. And then, for some reason, got herself married to a boy in the big class called Penaluna. Yes, Penaluna. The one with the onions in the garden. Strange, that. She was the first to smoke and drink, along with that boy, Penaluna. Not me. No. I was the nice one. But she became the nice one, out of her handicap. And I became the bad one, out of a sense of forgetting.

'My lovely Lois, so good with children, and so good with the cooking. I am looking forward to the time when you will cook for us all again.'

A weak smile, one of my best ones. So ill, so ill now.

I was just a girl when we moved away from Sheepwash in Devon. And came here to form a lasting friendship with my dear Marjorie.

I must walk up the hill and see her husband, Penaluna. I must just do that some of these days, as they do say. No, I am afraid of that. Of what? Of what I will find up there in the Crescent. Afraid he will be not alone, or will be alone with the onions, but dirty, very unclean about his person, about the house. Well, it happens. How it happens. God gave me the children, and I gave nothing back. Was not required to, not yet. In the chapel, the rain falling on the roof, staring through the bars of the pew. The Infant Roll Call. Death on its own plate. I was only seven years old, already tall for my years and skinny, very skinny, with large white socks, crying, crying as the rain fell. Because I did not want to turn again. Because I did not want to turn. To Jesus. And later, much later, walking down Chapel Hill, feeling the winged chariot behind me, fear gripping my young bones, knowing there was more to pregnancy than loving. You came close to death; so close he brushed you with his wing-tip. The eyes half closed in the weeks before the baby came. And the eyes wide open at the time, at that awful time. But now, it seems like a job to be done. A good old spring-clean with hope that one doesn't fall off the ladder. Into the void. And Marjorie, whose voice sometimes modulated like that of the cat. The cat's inquisitive voice. Don't be afraid, Lois, the land did not rise up against you when you were pregnant at first, and it won't rise up against you this time. But this time I will be buried. Under the Devon soil. No, under the black soil here. What is wrong with me. I am not going to die. Not me. I am not going to die. Not now. Not this time. I am the Mother of a new family, Tage and me. An Af Klercker to take the place of old Mrs Af Klercker. Never mind. And the trouble. And the care. And the time it took to begin to sort it all out, this life, this adulthood, or whatever they choose to call it. And all I can hear now, from the bedroom next door to mine is, yes, the squeaks of the Commodore. The boys and their games. Not the sort that we knew, dear, no, not the sort we knew. The home computer, invented by Satan. There he goes, my dear one Jerry, the fastest of them all. Has taken out the Islamic alliance, the world is uninhabitable because of radiation and Pakistan is still ordering missiles, though it was wiped out five minutes ago. Ah well, that's that, then. 'World Peace' it's no doubt called. The idea being to stay in the game. Like all games. To stay in the game. There's the rub. More tea, Tage, my dear Tage? Keep your options open.

CHAPTER 13

I don't want to get out of the bed. Not now, not ever. The children all around me, wondering what to do, waiting for my direction. Just go to school, children. You are due back at school now.

Sounds of a house in suspension. He left a note beside my corner of the bed. Saying, I think it is best. Whatever I do is never right. And it frightens me. I felt his kiss on my forehead, soft, sentimental, inadequate to this trouble of mine. A total, total stranger. I was just looking through a tunnel at him. Then he left me and he was gone. That is all I can say about it, Doctor. Then he left me and he was gone again.

Sitting here in bed worrying. They think I will get up out of bed if he goes away. Now that he has gone away. Tee hee, Tage. It will take more than your departure to get me up. My only fear, dear, is the social worker, who will take my children away from me in the spring. But even that doesn't matter. Davey's children will survive. They are strong and wily like their father. They will go on without me. They will have to.

But it is pleasant here, I will say that for it. Very pleasant. Mild for the time of the year. It was love, you know, back there in Sweden. When we got married. Not all that long ago. But now it's goodbye. Not that Tage knows it. No. Tage thinks that we shall be together again in a few days, when I have come to my senses. Egged on by the doctor, and the Viking folklore. But now, I will never go back. It is a question of will, you see, of what is apt. I have gained in strength and power this day. I will never go back. And Tage will. Me with my cream handbag and navy blue suit. Or the other way around.

'Well, hello there, Lois.'

'I am leaning out of the window, hoping to get some air.'

'Eh, what?'

'I am leaning out of the window, hoping to get some air in my lungs.'

Penaluna stands, cap in his hands. Rolling it around. Bereft of his Marjorie. And oh, the things I could say at this juncture. Which would not be heard, no, nor understood very well, but dimly, darkly.

What she wrote to me from her bed in London was that she was not well, not well at all. Had got something, something terrible. And that Penaluna, of all people in the world, was not to know. It would do no good.

And that man now stood in front of me. Harmless, all-forgiving, all-seeing, all-wise. Who would have understood instantly, and would have comprehended fully. Being a man, not of the world, not of the farm, as Davey was, with the narrow-minded prejudice, not of the park, with the Doctor's woolly ambition, not of deadly middle class Swedish farming stock, but being a man. Just a Cornish man. And I saw it in an instant, in an overwhelming moment. Marjorie had been the luckiest of all. She had had Penaluna, and I had had nothing. Air, vapour was my lot. I had had nothing. And now I was reaping the whirlwind. As was Marjorie.

Penaluna, the husband, staring up at my window, lost and bewildered. Above all, bewildered. You mean to say, he was saying in his mind, that he has gone and left you and the kids, all alone now, at this time. Good God, Lois, he was saying. He mustn't do that. When Davey would have done it without a thought. Especially if it was a choice between me and the sheep at lambing time. Might lose an ewe if you weren't careful. But a wife you could find anywhere. A wife cost very very little.

So there he was, standing beneath the window, feeling a bit silly and looking a bit daft, and I sorrowed for him then, yes sorrowed. Sorry for myself and sorry for my children. And I saw a nobility in him, in Penaluna. For the first time in my life. I respected a man. And it felt good.

But Marjorie: I could not tell him. I put my head in my hands, my elbows on the window-sill, and I wept. I wept for us all, but mostly for Marjorie and Penaluna. Because this was just another tragedy. Brought on by innocence. And that, I did not want to witness. Not in this frame of mind, with Tage now gone, and the crust hardening around my heart.

The ease of the early summer. The way she had gone on the train and left Toldhu Close. I had been glad for her. What a lark that had been. Good for her. Never been anywhere in her life before. Good to get away from that old deadbeat, Penaluna. Yes. And now this had happened. And I was in no condition to look for her and bring her back to die here. I would have to tell him and I could not. She did not want it.

'Lois?'

I know what that sound now means.

'I wondered if you heard from my wife.'

And still I find myself crying endlessly, strangely without pain, my tears dropping on the window-sill. Penaluna must surely know by now, and I have betrayed my old friend, whom I encouraged to ruin herself like a fool. It was like the end of a world and the beginning of another one. The new one not as good as the one before.

And through the tears I see Penaluna coming up the small path to my front door.

Dear Lord God, help me out, for I am guilty now. And Penaluna will be suffering for my misdeeds with regard to his wife. 'I never meant to, I never meant to,' will be my theme here.

In this empty afternoon, standing by my door and ringing my bell. I pulled the hospital dressing-gown around me and walked downstairs for the first time in many, many weeks.

Stepping inside, and speaking to me. Cap in hand. You see, you was her friend, for years, even in school, and I thought that, well, perhaps, you might. Have heard from her. But there was no sound, no comfort from me. I saw that as though I were him, Penaluna. Like the Heavens, I had nothing to say at this juncture. And he crumpled up, in the tiny hallway made for dwarfs. He just fell down.

And the sun kept beating down upon Toldhu Estate, and the veins stood out on my neck. I felt sick as a dog. I had brought all of this about. There had been nothing wrong with their joint life. They were two Cornish people living in Pixie Land in their traditional way, planting their onions and heaving up and down the road to the Spar shop. Timeless.

I brought down a letter from the upstairs room. One which said how much she enjoyed life in the Capital. How generous Londoners were. He read it beside the sink in the kitchen.

> *'I shall be alright because his sister will be coming.'*

> *'In a place called the Connawt which sounds a bit Irish to me.'*

> *'I could live down in Tremarle and sail down to get my fish and chips in Gweek if I had the money in Cornwall I am earning here.'*

I do not know what to say to Penaluna. He neither accuses nor shows a temper. But stands and looks miserable. There's nothing bad but thinking makes it so. For years I woke up at four, thinking of Davey going off to the dairy, thinking of me. The only time in the pre-dawn, when we communed once more again. Or was that just an illusion on my part? Or on his? They say that we all may be an illusion of the universe. I do not doubt it now.

There was one thought that came into my mind, time and time again, in the pre-dawn, and was remembered now, with Penaluna in the small hall-way. The golden countryside of the mind had darkened to grey. And was darkening further. Even as I stood and looked at Penaluna. And I blamed myself for all that had happened to my friend, and to Penaluna, her quiet husband, whom I had not known at all, whose furniture was being ruined in my lounge, because I had wreaked a kind of revenge on the Swede. Without cause, without cause.

And I could, even then, hear my own voice say, 'Marjorie's mixer is very useful to me.' Enlightened self-interest.

Penaluna did not smile.

'Let me see her letter, for God's sake.'

This was not a Tage, nor a Davey.

'I don't know where they are now. She is doing well, very well, I know. You will be proud of her.'

Prowling down the passage, looking for his wife's letters to me. Obsessed. I did not want the man wandering around my house, then. Almost wished the protection of Tage back in the house. Strange how a man knows when one's territory has been deserted by another. In the kitchen, by the refrigerator, he almost fell. But took a yellow chair and sat down on it by the table.

'Leave me alone. It hurts too much.'

'I don't think you 'ave any right, Lois, to talk about hurtin' too much. You encouraged her to go Lunnun. 'Twas too far. Too far. An' she was not at all prepared for un. Not at all prepared. Chris', Lois, I need yer 'elp. You do live in a dream.'

'Because I do not dare. Because I do not dare to turn again. Go away, Mr Penaluna. I can't help you. You will have to go now.'

'An' she wasn' prepared for un. Tha's why I did protect 'er. All the way along.'

'Ah yes.'

'What 'as 'appened to 'er, now, then?'

'Your wife, Marjorie? She went to London, got herself a decent job and went to work. Started to enjoy life instead of being mollycoddled and insulted here.'

'Shut up, Lois.'

'Agh, I'm sorry. It's these pills, and sitting alone in the house all day. Mollycoddled and insulted.'

'Yeah.' Tone lowered to an acceptable level.

'Not my fault, Mr Penaluna.'

'But Marjorie . . .'

'You still have your life.'

'Oh Lois. God, what is it now? Look, she was a beautiful woman. Vulnerable to your prattle. You know somethin' I don'.'

Penaluna's eyes, restless. Following a nightmare which was just coming into focus at the corner of the eye. Nothing to do. Sweet nothing to do about it now. All the damage was done. It was a matter of time now. Lois would not tell him. He had to find out. Or figure it out. That was just the way it was now.

'No!' He was clutching the table and howling, but silently.

'You're not going to blame me. You're not.'

'No, no. Not blame you. I'm gwoin now. Just let me get my breath. Really, Lois.'

'Go, Penaluna. I can't cope with it.'

The baby stirred in the belly. And she realised now, suddenly, that this was the first time he had shown his presence for a long time. That he was still alive after all. That was what it had been all these days. She had not heard from the baby. There had been a silence from the stomach. No personality conflicting with her own. Somewhere, in the darkness of the upper room, she had thought that he was dead, the little, silent stranger. And he wasn't.

Many times, though when the doctor probed about, there had been no suggestion he was dead. The man had simply stated that she was nuts. Quite nuts. Fit to be put away. And that was how it was, and that was how it was going to be. From that time forward, Nuts. Lois had done it. Lois had finally cracked. Well, it was having all those children, and that Swede for a husband. That was what it was. But nobody knew. Not really. Not yet. Nohow.

'I won't be blamed for what happened to Marjorie. She may be your wife, but she is my dearest friend. We went to school together.'

'Look, Lois, I 'ave to say this: I went to the same bleddy school.'

Lois gave up the thin, determined look. This was a husband, but not one of hers, past or present. She could give it up now. She could relax into the reality of that much.

What day was it now? A Monday. The children were at school, at their new schoolbooks. This was a new term for them. This was the end of the term for Lois.

Thanks to God, the creator of all things new and old, the baby would be out soon. No doubt about it.

A fine autumn Monday morning. With Penaluna in the kitchen and Tage in Flen. Marjorie in Lunnun and the boys at school. All was well with the world after all, then. Nothing to do but make yer friend Penaluna a cup of tea. And have one herself. Make the kettle sing.

What would they call the new one, Tage Af Klercker and his wife, now? Where would the dear thing be christened? In Sweden or in Cornwall? Ah what fun. The beginning of a life; the outset of a lifetime.

What was Penaluna doing now, then? Plenty of gardening? Getting things ready for the winter? Weeding the paths? Oh? Repairing the paths! Well, well, well. What a job, on the estate, with the finest row of onions this side of the viaduct allotments. It was wonderful, really, what one could do with a bed of onions. What they did for the soul ~ and for the soil, come to that.

Can you see that my heart longs for things to come right with Marjorie? But I cannot tell you, Penaluna. That your wife is going to die of this adventure. What shall I say to you instead?

CHAPTER 14

By stealth, driven by some instinct, Lois got friendly with Stanley Arthur Penaluna, and somehow, it came about that the gruff old devil came to tea every evening. And sat at the tea-table with the children, his cap and boots in the hall, and the entire little family began to laugh at his fine, clean jokes. It seemed that Marjorie had, after all, picked a winner in her life, but had not had the experience to spot him for a winner. And Lois had been too blinkered to see it either. Thus she had put her friend into unnecessary danger and had started the long process of killing her by sending her to London by her fine talk.

Or, that was how it seemed to Lois, talking to Penaluna comfortably over tea, whilst the baby grew a little inside her and put on a bit of weight in preparation for its first days in the world. Indeed, so full of spirit was Lois now that Penaluna's company was a joy and it seemed that nothing could or would ever depress her again. Not before the birth: not after the birth. Before long, too, gruff old Penaluna had begun to appear no longer old, just gruff. And cosy: very, very cosy. Penaluna seemed the sort of person they had all been looking for in their lives, the boys and Lois. Tage was forgotten. He was nothing to them, anyway, apart from having a remote connection with the coming baby. Well ~ that was how it all appeared, or might have appeared to an outsider, if an outsider had been allowed a peep into their lives.

Nobody was allowed inside their lives, though. Lois hummed and sang her way through the days, and admitted easily to herself that Penaluna was a dear, a fine old contrast to that awful Tage person, who had been nothing but a blight on their lives. A mere father of the baby to come, and that was all. Penaluna, on the other hand, was welcomed, or would have been welcomed if he had had the inclination, both day and evening. That was how it was in Toldhu Close now. Lois was so glad to have a friend. He talked about the garden, in warm, lambent tones, his voice soft and passionate of his onions and other growing things.

The only thing that bothered Lois at all was her premature vision of her dead friend, Marjorie. And Marjorie could not yet be dead. There was a lifetime of illness to be borne before Marjorie might be allowed to die. But there it was. She could not tell Penaluna about it. It was the only thing that blighted the platonic friendship. Or threatened to.

And the sun shone down on Toldhu Estate on Wednesdays and Fridays and Tuesdays and Sundays for a couple of hours in the day. Whenever it felt like it. And one Monday, Penaluna drove her down to the hospital in the van, where a girl in an overall said to wait, please wait for a wheelchair, but Lois didn't wait and dragged herself into the lift and on to the ward and before anybody could remove her grey raincoat he came out, the new one, like a bag of squashed tomatoes, stunned and angry, with the staff shouting and dragging at Penaluna to go and look, look, with Penaluna screwing his cap around and backing off saying he was only a neighbour he wasn't the father it wasn't right or decent he was only the van driver and now the front seat was probably ruined with amniotic fluid he would have to go and clean it out. And later, Doctor David John poked his head around the door, saying hello Lois, can you feel this? And later again, the children came and stood around the bed, silent, sucking a lolly.

Upon that day, the sun wore a black armband as he slipped down, down beyond that place where nobody goes. And as he fell and paused, poised above oblivion, it flashed green as it fell into the great ocean.

But nobody minded, nobody noticed, because after a period of darkness, tomorrow he would rise again over Toldhu Estate. The daisies would open and every mower would be out there on the lawns, cutting and mowing. The diggers would dig a hole for a fishpond. Window latches would open. Earth would be churned up over spring leaves. One or two onions would be pulled.

And a pair of girls from Reservoir Road would slip on a thin cardigan and nip down into the granite town, and stuff a Piggy Burger and banter with the Af Klercker boys.